To Brandi

Thank you For your Support
Have A Wonderful, Glorious,
Joyful Day 9-19-2023 Q-DAB

Text Copyright © 2023 by Q-DAB

All rights reserved. No part of this publication may be reproduced, distributed, or transmitted in any form or by any means, including photocopying, recording, or other electronic or mechanical methods without the prior written permission of the publisher. For permission requests, solicit the publisher via the address below.

SUSU Entertainment LLC
P.O. Box 1621
Cypress, TX 77410
www.susuentertainmentllc.com
susuentertainmentllc@gmail.com

Printed in the United States of America

Name: Q-DAB, Author

Title: | Love or Lust: An Inspiring Story Filled with Compassion, Romance, Heartbreak, Faith, and Love

Summary: Realistic fictional stories about a young woman's journey of finding joy, happiness, faith, and true love.

Identifiers:
ISBN: 978-1-956292-22-0 **(paperback)**
ISBN: 978-1-956292-23-7 (hardcover)

Subjects: | Be Intentional in Your Prayers | Have Faith | Trust God

Book Cover Design © 2023 by SUSU Entertainment LLC

LOVE OR LUST

AN INSPIRING STORY FILLED WITH COMPASSION, ROMANCE, HEARTBREAK, FAITH, AND LOVE

By: Q-DAB

Volume 1

TABLE OF CONTENTS

Chapter 1..It All Started in the Garden

Chapter 2..Love or Lust

Chapter 3.......................................The Secret Life of a Crush

Chapter 4......................................The Unexpected Blessing

Chapter 5.....................................A Customer's Connection

Chapter 6...................................Mr. Tall Dark and Handsome

Chapter 7......................................The Pretty Redbone Waitress

Chapter 8.......................................What's in the Briefcase?

Chapter 9..........................Looking Good and Feeling Good

Chapter 10..The Interrogation

Chapter 11..................................Happy Birthday First Date

Chapter 12..................................The Truth Will Set You Free

Chapter 13......................................Shop Until You Drop

Chapter 14……….......………....…Guess Who's Coming to Dinner?

Chapter 15…………………...........................Bible Study Blessings

Chapter 16……….........................………….Nikki's Water Baptism

Chapter 17……….…….......................……The Greatest Gift for Marcus

Chapter 18……….……….....................………New Beginnings of Love

Chapter 19……….….................……………In Sickness and in Health

Chapter 20…………..........................…………...Tricks of the Enemy

Chapter 21……….….............………….Welcome To Pleasure Palace

Chapter 22……….…….........................…….. Rest in Heavenly Peace

Chapter 23………….................…. ..………....…The Wedding Ceremony

Chapter 24……….……….................................…….......Church Folks

Chapter 25……….….............................………….God's Perfect Timing

PREFACE

You will see in the book as you read that there are weak links. Some of the characters will continue to stay weak and others will seek forgiveness from God for the sins that were committed. By choosing sin, we stray far from God. The world offers only a craving for us to see. When we lust after others, we are taking from them but when we love, we are giving to them. We must always seek guidance from the Holy Spirit.

In the living translation, as we read God's word, the Holy Spirit speaks to us in many wonderful ways. It speaks to us, convict us, encourage us, and strengthens us. You can say that the Holy Spirit causes us to come alive through God's word every time we read it.

We serve a compassionate, loving, and gracious God. He never gets tired of bearing the burdens for his children. The love we have for God will direct us back on the right track of salvation. We should never allow Satan to cause us to sin by the lust of the flesh, lust of the eye, and the pride of life, it is not of the Father but of the world. [1 John 2:16]

We must pray for restoration, clarity in the chaos, and ask for forgiveness. Ask God to refresh you with his grace and mercy and renew a steadfast spirit within you.

INTRODUCTION

Nikki had always been infatuated with her childhood crush Jonathan, often fantasizing about them becoming a couple. As a young adult, she got the opportunity to tell him how she felt but after some shocking news and a tragedy, Nikki realized that her heart may have been filled with lust not love. After learning about an unexpected blessing, Nikki decided to move far away to start a new beginning.

She often prayed for God to bless her with a God-fearing, tall, dark, and handsome man with a briefcase that would be good to her and for her. At the diner where Nikki worked, she met a guy named Bradford that fit the exact description of what she had been praying for. As their relationship grew, Bradford was very transparent in what he wanted, even offering her a key to his heart.

Nikki cared deeply for Bradford, her passion for him often went into overdrive, but Bradford stayed strong and didn't allow the temptation of his flesh to become weak. Bradford was the perfect gentleman, but Nikki was scared to make a commitment, fear of things she witnessed in her past. She wanted to make sure that their relationship was based on love not lust. Nikki knew that God may not always bless you with what you want, but what you need. Bradford didn't leave anything for the imagination, but there was still a mystery about him that Nikki was determined to find out.

IT ALL STARTED IN THE GARDEN

In the beginning, in the Garden of Eden Satan found the weakest link which happened to be Eve. [Genesis 3:6]. Satan started communicating with her causing her to doubt their creator, God. Satan had Eve feeling that she and Adam were missing out on something that God didn't want them to know. Adam and Eve weren't in need of anything, they didn't even have to worry about clothes. Once the doubt had set in, Satan knew her eye gate would be opened. What you allow to enter through your eye gates will seep into your mind and eventually into your heart. That's how Satan used Eve to persuade her to eat from the tree. God told them that the Garden of Eden was their home, the only thing that was forbidden was the tree of the knowledge of good and evil.

Eve ate then she gave it to Adam to eat, and he knew that they were doing wrong. He ate because he did not want to sleep on the other side of the Garden of Eden. They ate and that's when sin came on the scene. Lust of the flesh, lust of the eye, and the pride of life [1 John 2:16]. Now we know how sin came on the scene and it is up to us to make the choice, will it be love or lust. Will we be the weak link or the strong link in life?

To be the strong link, we must connect to the Most High God. We must embrace the Holy Spirit to direct our path. We are going to sin in this sinful world from choices that we make. When we sin, we must remember where our help comes from, and that help is from God.

LOVE OR LUST

It was January 23, 1999, Nikki's life started on a journey that was unbeknown to her. There's an old saying that the only thing constant is change. She was a young lady that had very high expectations for her life, but things were not going the way she had dreamed her life would be with Jonathan, her night and shining armor. Nikki didn't realize that the boy, Jonathan, she had a little girl crush on, quickly grew into a teenage infatuation. As a young adult she would still be having these same feelings. Nikki didn't understand if these feelings were love or lust? Her focus was on how she was going to let Jonathan know how she felt about him for a very long time. She knew that eventually the opportunity would present itself.

Nikki had no idea that her wish would be granted sooner than she even imagined. She was excited that she was invited to her friend's wedding. Nikki loved going to weddings, but never wanted to be front and center when it was time for the bride to throw her bouquet. She felt she was too young for marriage. Nikki entered through the church doors looking like a beautiful princess. She was immediately escorted by an usher who seated her on the bride's side of the sanctuary. She sat down and started to mingle with the other guests while waiting for the wedding to begin. The wedding ceremony started, and the preacher came out with the groom and best man. Nikki almost fell out of her seat when she saw the best man. She could hardly believe her eyes, it was Jonathan, her long-time secret crush standing beside the Groom!

All she could think was wow! There he was, Jonathan, the one and only that she had had these feelings for as long as she could remember. The question she kept asking herself, is this love or lust? Nikki's emotions were all over the place. She sat there with the wedding guests and started to daydream. Her mind had wondered many miles away. Was this the night that she would let Jonathan know how she felt about him since she was a child? The music started to play for the wedding party to start entering the room, Nikki quickly came back to reality. The wedding was beautiful, exactly what a bride would want on her wedding day. Nikki was so happy for her friend and for herself, because she felt this would be the perfect opportunity for her and Jonathan to meet.

Everyone headed over to the reception to wait for the wedding party. Nikki drove to the reception alone all discombobulated, wondering if Jonathan had a date. If he did have a date, then she would have a change of plans letting him know her feelings for him. Nikki was driving without paying attention and was almost in a car accident. Nikki realized that she had to stay focused and not let her feelings allow her to not be able to function properly. On her way to the reception venue, she gathered herself and her thoughts. Nikki got out of her car and walked gracefully across the parking lot.

Once she entered the venue, she looked around for a place to sit, front and center so she would be close to the wedding party and watch Jonathan's every move. It was time for the bride and groom to do their first dance, as soon as the DJ said that the guest could join the bride and groom on the dance floor, Nikki was at the wedding party table asking Jonathan to dance. He immediately said yes, and Nikki was one happy little girl in a grown woman's body. They danced and danced the night away.

The wedding party had left the head table, so Nikki invited Jonathan to sit with her at her table. She smiled all the way to the table thinking this was what she had been waiting for. They were seated and he asked her if she would like something to drink. She said, "Yes, you can surprise me!" Nikki started gathering her thoughts so she would be able to tell him how she felt about him since she was a little girl. When Jonathan returned with the drinks she told him, and he acted very surprised. When he found out how Nikki felt about him, he had mixed feelings because all he remembered was the little girl that he had grown up around and the person sitting at the table with him was no little girl anymore.

The night was about to end, Nikki was sitting at the table looking very beautiful, when suddenly Jonathan asked her for her phone number. He told her that he would be calling her soon. "Okay, I will be waiting patiently." Nikki said. Before he got up from the table he leaned over and kissed Nikki on the cheek, later returning to the table where the wedding party had been sitting.

Nikki thanked the bride and groom for the invite and to their beautiful wedding. She gave them a hug and told them that she was getting ready to leave. Nikki got in her car and began to process what happened at the reception with Jonathan. She told herself that Jonathan would know how she felt about him before the night was over and she was happy her mission was accomplished. Nikki headed home with a smile on her face wondering when he would call. The next few days passed, and he had not called, that evening the phone rang and it was Jonathan asking her for a date. She told him yes!

THE SECRET LIFE OF A CRUSH

The next day he picked her up for their first date and told her that the movie he wanted to take her were an hour away. Nikki told him that it would be fine. Jonathan took her to a restaurant to have dinner first. This was something that Nikki had fantasized about for years. Every date they had; Jonathan took Nikki out of town.

One night, Nikki asked Jonathan why they had to leave their home city to drive an hour away. Jonathan quickly changed the subject, saying, "I have a special evening planned for us." That night he took Nikki to a very extravagant restaurant with a hotel and mall connected. After dinner he took Nikki to the mall to do some shopping. Little did she know, they would end up at a lingerie shop and he picked her out something that he wanted her to wear. Nikki didn't say a word, just taking notes on the man that she assumed she loved dearly.

After leaving the lingerie shop, they ended up at the front desk of the hotel. Jonathan gave his name, and the desk clerk gave him the room keys. Nikki still observing the man that she loved but clearly didn't know. As they entered the room, there sat a bottle of champagne on ice. Jonathan was full of surprises, making it a night to remember. He had thought of everything for a romantic night. Nikki still had not received an answer to the question she had asked him earlier that day about why they had to go out of town for their dates.

Nikki thought to herself, *all this that he has done for me, but it is still not in our home city*. This did not sit well with her, but she remained quiet. The night was something that she had been dreaming of with Jonathan all her young adult life, however, she was not feeling the way she assumed she would feel. There was no passion, it seemed that he was pleasing himself more than pleasing her. Nikki wasn't truly ready to have sex with Jonathan because it was their first date and she really wanted to get to know him better.

Their intimacy wasn't mutual, Nikki just went along because she had been infatuated with Jonathan for years and he had showered her with a lovely first date. No one should feel because someone has wined and dined them that they owe them something in return. Your body is your temple and should be preserved for that special someone. The next morning, Nikki got up early to take a shower reminiscing about what happened last night. She was concerned because it didn't feel like they shared love with each other, it was more like lust.

Lust is purely a sexual attraction, spending most of your time with a partner being physically intimate, having little interest in their life outside of the bedroom, having different morals and values. Lust is an intense feeling that dominates our thoughts and can drive us to do things against our better judgement. There was still some mystery about this man that Nikki didn't quite understand. The next morning, she got dressed and woke Jonathan up and asked him to take her home.

Jonathan took her home and before she got out of the car, she told him she had a great time and that she would call him the next week. She leaned over and gave him a big kiss on his lips and said, "Goodbye Jonathan." Nikki had no idea that it would be her last time seeing Jonathan alive and well. Before Nikki had a chance to call Jonathan like she told him she would, he was in a fatal car accident that killed him on the scene. When Nikki heard this on the news she was devastated.

While watching TV, the news reporter told the story of the accident and the people that Jonathan was leaving behind, his family and fiancé. When Nikki heard fiancé, she stood straight to her feet! She could not finish listening to the reporter. Nikki was so upset with Jonathan and even more upset because she could not confront him about not being honest with her. She started to back track their dating and she remembered the last night they were together, she asked Jonathan why they always had to date away from their home city, and he changed the subject. Nikki yelled, "Wow!" She was in total disbelief.

Nikki started pacing the floor back and forth. How could I have been so naïve? She carried a heavy burden, but with the strength of her faith, she continued with her life. She didn't go to the funeral to pay her respect, because she had no respect for someone that had taken advantage of her and wasn't honest. Nikki tried to block this tragedy from her mind and started focusing on making the next day a new beginning.

THE UNEXPECTED BLESSING

One day Nikki was putting on one of her favorite outfits and noticed that she had gained some weight, not giving any thought to the weight gain, she went to her closet to get another outfit. Nikki enjoyed spending quality time with herself and was treating herself to dinner at one of her favorite restaurants. She arrived and was so excited. The waiter seated her, while waiting, she enjoyed the sweet melodies of a live band.

Nikki could smell the food aroma so vividly, it smelled so good, but suddenly Nikki rushed to the bathroom and leaned over one of the commodes throwing up profusely. After she was finished, she rinsed her mouth trying to figure out what had just happened. When she got back to her seat her server walked up to the table. Nikki told him that she would not be ordering anything because she had a sick spell. The server jokingly said, "Well Ms. are you pregnant?" Nikki said, "No!" She quickly left the restaurant.

Nikki had not even given the thought of being pregnant until the server had asked her that question. She started to think about her weight gain and now she's throwing up from the smell of good food. The next day Nikki went to the clinic for a pregnancy test and yes, she was pregnant! Sadly, it was the same number of months that Jonathan had died. She was pregnant by a man that had kept their relationship a secret because he had a fiancé and now, he is dead. Nikki was in total shock! What was she going to do? Her son Marcus was born, and Nikki moved to the town where her sister lived in South Georgia.

Being a single Mom was something that Nikki was not familiar with, but she knew she could do it with the help from her sister. Once Nikki got all settled with a job, life became much better for her. Marcus was such a joy to the family, and he was growing so fast. Nikki told her sister Lois that she had found an apartment and that she and Marcus would be moving out. Nikki was a waitress and that is how she supported herself and took good care of her son, he was not wanting for anything. She made sure that the absence of his sperm donor was not missed since he was deceased. Nikki put the love for her child and the love she had for his dad and promised herself that she would cherish his memory forever by making the best life she could for her and her son.

Nikki never fathomed being a single Mom. Her life was often overwhelmed and compromised, from coping with loss, having to stay strong, anxiety over money, maintaining a work/life balance, and having to deal with the stresses of making decisions alone for her son. This was not the life she expected to live. Through the tragedy of losing the love of her life, she was very thankful for the support she constantly received from her sister and her family. Without their undeniable love, she didn't know how she would be able to make it through.

A CUSTOMER'S CONNECTION

Nikki had been a waitress for many years and although it wasn't her dream job, she was happy that it paid the bills. Everyday consisted of a lot of going back and forth serving customers drinks, meals, clearing the tables, and helping the kitchen staff, a very high pace environment. It was a Wednesday night and Nikki was getting ready to end her shift. The restaurant door opened, and two handsome young men walked in. Tammy, the hostess greeted them at the door and led them to their table. Nikki watched Tammy as she passed up all the tables and took straight into the glass house, Nikki's station. Tammy walked over to Nikki and said, "You have customers in your station." Nikki gave Tammy the evil eye and asked, "Why did you put them in my station when you know all I had to do was roll silverware and then I could go home?" Tammy looked at Nikki with a big smile and said, "Girl, I have my reasons."

Nikki told Tammy she didn't care what kind of reason she had, she was tired and was ready to go home. Nikki went ahead and sucked it up, smiled and prepared her tray as she put the water and silverware for her customers and headed to her glass house station. She cheerfully greeted them, "Hi, my name is Nikki, and I will be your waitress tonight. "Are you guys ready to order?" Nikki asked. They replied, "We're not ready yet, but do you have any specials today?" "Yes, the Wednesday special is inside the menu on the right," Nikki replied. While they were looking, Nikki was standing there checking them out from head to toe, thinking these guys are handsome.

After being in La La land for a minute she asked if they wanted to see the lunch menu for more ideas. They both stated,

"Yes!" She noticed it wasn't on their table, so she left to go and get the lunch menu for her customers. While they sat and waited the guys seemed quite smitten with their waitress whispering on how good she looked and the sound of her sweet heavenly voice, mimicking her saying, "You guys ready to order?"

Nikki got back to the table with the menus and her customers were already ready to order. Nikki couldn't believe after she had walked all the way to the other side of the restaurant, they were immediately ready to order. She wished they had ordered before she left, it would have saved time, but she continued to give them great customer service, while smiling and taking their orders as if nothing was wrong. The guys started to have small talk saying, "Nikki you must not be from around here asking us are you guys ready to order. Normally, around here we always hear people saying, "Yawl." Nikki said, "I am from the Midwest, Wisconsin." Nikki truly enjoyed conversing with the guys, reflecting in her mind, *I guess it's not so bad having to stay longer waiting on these handsome young men.*

As the two young men were talking, she heard that the tall guy's name was Brad and his friend's name was Tommy. Nikki took their orders and went to get their drinks, then she went to the break room where everyone usually gathers. Nikki told her co-workers that it was two handsome young men in her station thanks to Tammy. Nikki gave Tammy a look, then a quick wink of approval. Tammy smiled and said, "Girl, I told you I did it for a reason." Nikki started describing them to the girls. There's one that's tall, dark, and handsome, about 6'4 in height. Nikki reminisced about Jonathan, her secret crush that had gotten killed in a car accident, because he was about 6'4. The girls said, "Nikki what are you going to do if you and him get together, hug his ankles?" Nikki was only 5 feet tall. Nikki chuckled, "Ha, ha, ha very funny! If we decide to become a couple, I guess I will have to learn how to climb a tree." The girls laughed hysterically. I've already had practice with my son's dad because he was about the same height.

"I have to go ladies," Nikki said. "I have to take my customers their drink orders." Nikki started rushing to the front to take their drinks to them. She took the drinks when Bradford joked and said, "We thought we were going to have to send a search party to find our waitress." Nikki smiled and said, "I am so sorry it took longer than expected to get back with your sweet tea." Bradford added, "This tea should be very good and sweet long as it took to get here." Nikki told him that she used a little tender, loving, care (TLC) while putting ice in the glasses and pouring the tea. Bradford was being flirty and so was she. Nikki scurried back to get their food from the kitchen. The flirty behavior between her and Bradford made her feel all warm and fuzzy inside.

As the guys waited, Bradford told Tommy that he was going to ask Nikki for her phone number before they left the restaurant because he wanted to get to know her. Just as he was saying that Nikki walked up with their food asking them if they needed anything else. Tommy said, "My friend needs something," by that time Brad kicked Tommy Keys under the table. Nikki asked, "What do you need?" Brad responded, "More tea please." Brad asked with a smile on his face, "Can we get it before we are finished eating?" Nikki said, "Yes sir," and started walking away when something really shocked her, she saw both guys praying over their food before they started eating. Nikki hurried back to the break room to tell the girls that the guys that were in her station were God-fearing because she saw them praying over their food before they started eating.

Nikki went back to their table with a pitcher of sweet tea and filled their glasses. She asked if everything was all right, and they replied, "Yes, everything is fine." Nikki left a picture of tea on their table and went to the back and started back rolling the silverware as she patiently waited for her customers to finish eating so she could go home. Nikki was thankful that her brother-in-law and her sister Lois were able to watch her son since she had to work overtime. Nikki went back to the table and asked, "Would you guys like to order some dessert?" Bradford, the tall one gave Nikki a look like he was saying you could be my dessert. This caused Nikki to blush uncontrollably.

They told her that everything was good and that they would pass on the dessert this time. Nikki wrote up the bill and gave it to them. She asked one more time if they needed anything else. Bradford got up his nerves and said, "Yes, I need something else Nikki." She asked, "What else do you need?" He replied, "Your phone number." Nikki smiled and said, "I don't give out my phone numbers to strangers. You may be one of those serial killers, and besides that I don't even know your name. Although she had already overheard them talking earlier and knew both of their names.

"I know that I am a stranger, but I am a good stranger." The tall one said. Look into these eyes and tell me if I look like one of those serial killing people. Nikki looked into his eyes as she thought that she was going to melt all over the floor. His eyes were so sexy! Nikki stated, "We haven't formally met each other, and you are wanting my phone number. His friend agreed and said, "Man that's right get on him asking for your phone number and he haven't even introduced himself." The tall one replied, "Be cool man, I'm getting ready to introduce myself." Sorry Nikki, my name is Bradford and my friend's name is Tommy Keys, they all shook hands. Nikki said, "I saw you guys pray over your food before you ate, do you guys attend the Bible College that is here in town?" She was shocked how both replied quickly, "No!" "We attend the University in town, we're Art majors."

Nikki told them it was nice to see young men pray over their food in public. Bradford told Nikki, "You see, I'm not a bad guy, I would just like to get to know you better because you seem like a nice young lady." Nikki said, "I will give it to you." She pulled out a napkin and began writing her number down and gave it to him. He looked at it and said, "Could you please put your name on there too?" She wrote down Nikki C. Bradford asked, "What does the "C" stand for. She explained, "If I had wanted you to know what the C stood for, I would have written it down." Bradford said, "Sorry Miss C!" He chuckled and then told Tommy Keys; she is feisty, little pretty girl.

Thank you, Nikki for your phone number. You will be hearing from me soon. By that time, Tommy Keys told him that it was time to call it a night, my hubby duties are calling. "So, you are married?" Nikki asked. "Yes, ma'am!" My wife and I have three beautiful children. Tommy Keys happily replied. Are you married Bradford, "Well, umm just joking no, not yet." Bradford gave her a wink as he responded. All that time Nikki did not know that Tommy Keys was married with three children. She was happy that she was attracted to Bradford. Nikki told the guys to have a good night, as she had finished her shift, clocked out and went home.

MR. TALL DARK AND HANDSOME

Nikki went home that night feeling a little different from all the other nights after leaving work. She had a sparkle in her eyes and was feeling very excited inside. Nikki went home to her warm and cozy upstairs apartment filled with beautiful green plants, and a fun and spacious area where her son could learn and play. Before Nikki got ready for bed, she called her sister Lois to check on Marcus. When Lois answered the phone, she could immediately hear a different tone in her sister's voice. Lois said, "What's up Nikki, you are sounding all bubbly tonight." Nikki chuckled and asked, "How do you know that I am feeling pretty happy tonight?" "Whatever has you like this I am glad. "Ok sister, please tell me right now what it is!" Lois exclaimed.

Nikki ignored her sister's request and asked, "So how is Marcus?" "He is doing fine, he is asleep. I am waiting for you to tell me what's going on with you," said Lois. Nikki started explaining, "Lois, I met this guy tonight at work, he and his friend came to the restaurant for dinner. Tammy, the hostess put them in my station just when I was finishing up to go home, then she told me that she did it for a reason. Lois, I was glad that Tammy had put them in my station once I started to wait on them."

Nikki started to describe the guy that she was interested in named Bradford. He's tall, dark, and handsome, well-spoken, and well-groomed with a neatly cut fade. His friend's name was Tommy Keys, he is married with three children. Lois, Bradford, and I seemed to connect very well and later he asked for my phone number, and I gave it to him." "Wow, Nikki! He must have been some kind of guy for you to give him your phone number, because you have not been trying to let anyone in your life since you had Marcus," expressed Lois.

Lois added, "He may be the one since he has put some spark back into your life." "You may be right Lois, only time will tell about this handsome hawk," said Nikki. "Give Marcus a kiss for me and I'll talk with him on tomorrow, it's time for me to get ready for bed." "Love you and have a good night," added Nikki. She went into her bathroom to make her a hot bath. Her bathroom was decked out in beautiful bathroom décor to fit the perfect queen. Nikki's apartment was small but perfect for her and her son Marcus. She took pride in creating a unique oasis that they could call home. While her bath water was running, she lit her candles and turned off the lights, it was the perfect atmosphere to soak and relax in a hot bubble bath. Nikki took off her work clothes and stepped into her hot and steamy bubble bath, she laid her head back on her bath pillow and started thinking about what had happened at the restaurant.

Nikki couldn't stop thinking about her tall, dark, and handsome customer Bradford. His sexy eyes were mesmerizing. He had a beautiful smile with a gap in the middle of his top teeth which made her just tingle all over. To top it all off, he had a square-shaped head with a low-cut with waves that would make you seasick if you looked too long. Before she knew it, Nikki let out a scream of excitement. Thank you, Jesus! She couldn't believe how this man made her feel tingly all over, as if she was a young teenager excited about her first love. Nikki was daydreaming for so long that the water in the tub had turned cold. She quickly took her bath and got out of the tub pondering whether Bradford may be the one that she had been praying for to love and take care of her and Marcus.

THE PRETTY REDBONE WAITRESS

On the other side of town, Bradford was laying in his bed thinking about the pretty redbone waitress he had just met that had a body that was about 120 pounds about 5 feet tall with curves in all the right places. Although men are attracted to the physical first, her beauty shined beyond just her outer physic, he could tell that she had a pure heart. Nikki stayed on his mind throughout the night until the early morning, and all he could think about was her beautiful face, sexy voice, and her butt was so fine that it looked like it was breathing when she walked. Her smile was pretty and bright, she seemed to light up the entire room when she came to their table. Bradford was excited that someone so pretty and nice had given him her phone number. He laid in bed wondering, *is this the woman I have been praying for to be my wife?* He thought, *only time would tell*, then he rolled over and went to sleep.

The next morning Nikki's phone ranged; it was Bradford. He asked, "Good morning pretty lady, did you sleep well?" She said, "Yes I did, thanks for asking, but I'm sorry, who is this?" She really did know that it was Bradford, she was just trying to play hardball. He said, "This is Bradford, the guy you met last night at the restaurant. "You didn't think I was going to call, did you?" She said, "Yes, but not this soon." Bradford said, "I would like to see you today, if that's ok?" Nikki told him that she had an 11 to 7 shift. He told her that he would be at the restaurant for lunch and would request to be seated at her station. She said, "Okay I will see you later." Bradford responded, "Have a good morning pretty lady." Nikki got out of the bed with a radiant smile on her face, thinking to herself as she went to make her morning coffee, *Bradford is all right so far making my day this early in the morning.*

After she finished her coffee, she took her shower and started getting ready for work. She made sure that she put on the best body cream and perfume she had. Nikki put on the fragrance that would be intoxicating to Bradford because she wanted to smell her best and look her best when he saw her. Nikki applied her makeup, put her earrings on, styled her hair to make sure it was off her neck, and looked in the mirror and said, "You go girl!" At the restaurant your hair always had to be pinned up and if you are a cook, you must wear a hairnet.

Nikki was so excited that she got dressed two hours before work. She called her sister Lois, laughing as she answered the phone. "What has you so giggly this early morning?" Lois asked. Nikki answered, "Sister, Bradford called me this morning and asked when he would be able to see me again. I told him my work schedule for today and he said he was coming to the restaurant for lunch." Lois said, "That's good, but why are you laughing?" "Well sister, I got so excited that I was already dressed for work two hours early and you know that never happens." "Wow, Nikki! I see he has a positive effect on you. I love it!" Lois expressed. "Did Marcus get off to school okay this morning?" Nikki asked. "Yes, he did!" Lois said. Nikki said, "Thank you so much for helping the way that you do for me and Marcus. "Well little sister, I'm going to help you out as much as you need me to," expressed Lois.

Nikki was happy that she had a great support system. Having family support helps decrease parental stress, strengthens family ties, and improves outcomes for children. Nikki was very grateful for the love and support that she received from her sister and her family. "I guess I will get up and go to work now, love you sister, talk with you later," Nikki expressed. When Nikki got to work her coworkers asked why she was looking all pretty and smelling so good. Nikki always looked nice at work, but they quickly saw it was an extra effort that day that had her glowing. She told them when she woke up, this was how she decided to come to work today that's all. She tried to convince them by saying, "Girls, I do like to look good and smell good since I work all the time."

Shortly after that conversation, Tammy walked up, and all the girls started telling Tammy to look at Nikki and how pretty she looked today. Tammy told them that guy she met last night must be coming in today. Immediately they asked, "What guy?" Tammy told them that she had put two handsome guys in Nikki's station last night and Nikki had her eyes set on the tall one. Nikki said, "Hey Tammy that tall one would have a name, and it is Bradford, and yes, he will be in sometime today so put him in my station okay." The girls started screaming, saying, "He must be all that the way Nikki is acting!" Nikki responded, "Yes he is a good catch, and I intend on finding out if he is a keeper very soon."

One co-worker added, "Tammy mentioned that you didn't even want to wait on them last night." Nikki said, "Yes, I didn't. Sorry Tammy for giving you the evil eye." The ladies had to stop their chattering because it was about lunchtime, and it was busy. Nikki was taking drinks to her customers when the restaurant door opened. This tall, handsome man walked in with his light gray suit, white shirt starched to perfection, gray, white and royal blue paisley tie, and pocket square with royal blue snakeskin shoes carrying a black briefcase; it was Bradford. Nikki was so in awe; she almost dropped her tray.

Nikki just couldn't get over what a hunk Bradford was, and she was very happy that he wanted to get to know her. Tammy escorted Bradford to one of Nikki's empty tables. He waited patiently until she was able to make it over to his table to speak and give him a menu. She went to get the water, silverware, and a pitcher of sweet tea. Nikki went back to Bradford's table with a smile so big, you probably could count all 32's. She said, "Hi my name is Nikki, and I will be your waitress. I've already brought you a pitcher of sweet tea, would you like anything else to drink?" She asked. "No, the sweet tea is just what I wanted to drink, and you are looking beautiful today." Bradford said. "Thank you, Mr. Bradford," said Nikki. Bradford added, "I like your new hairstyle and you smell so good." "Wow you are full of compliments, thank you very much.

Are you ready to order?" Nikki asked. Nikki was still playing hardball. He said, "Yes!" She took the order and just as she was getting ready to walk away, she turned around and said, "You sure do look handsome today and your shoes are my favorite color, royal blue." She walked away smiling from ear to ear. When she put the order up the girls came over and asked, "Is that Bradford?" "Yes, it is!" Nikki exclaimed. Her co-workers said, "Girl, you better be glad he wasn't in my station last night." "Well, good thing he wasn't!" Nikki replied, as she walked off still smiling on her way to check on her other customers.

The table that Tammy put Bradford at was sitting at the end of Nikki's station. He was able to watch her all while she was taking care of her other customers, he did not take his eyes off her. Bradford was sitting there thinking about how Nikki was just like a breath of fresh air, a woman for his eyes only. He wanted to get to know all about her. She had captured his heart and he was very pleased. While he was in in fantasy world, Nikki walked up with his food. She said, "Mr. Bradford, here is your food." She laughed and asked, "What part of La La land did you go?" He smiled and said, "I don't know what part, but you were there." She asked, "Really? I was, and what was I doing in your La La land?" Bradford answered, "We were just getting to know each other." Nikki looked at him in astonishment and he quickly said, "Oh, no not like that! We went on a few dates." She responded, "Oh, okay." "Do you need anything else to go along with his meal," Nikki asked. He replied, "Everything is fine so far, thank you."

Nikki went back to the workstation where her coworkers were and told them to look over at Bradford's table and watch. They asked, "What are we watching for Nikki?" She said, "Just watch and see what he does." As they watched, Bradford slowly bowed his head and prayed over his food. Nikki told them that he was the kind of guy she would want to marry. If it wasn't him, at least someone just like him. Nikki went to Bradford's table and asked if he needed any more sweet tea. "No, thank you." Bradford asked, "How did you know I wanted sweet tea?" Nikki answered, "Well, the way you acted last night about the sweet tea, I just assumed that's what you wanted to drink today. He said, "Well, you assumed right!" Bradford and Nikki chuckled. Out of the blue, Bradford surprised Nikki by saying, "You know something young lady, I really do like you, even though I just met you." Nikki blushed and said, "You know you seem to be a pretty nice guy yourself, and yes I would like to get to know you too."

Nikki was very impressed in how Bradford bowed his head and thanked God for his food before he started eating. Bradford told her about a scripture from the Bible that he lives by, and it was Matthew 6:33. Nikki asked, "What does that scripture say?" He explained, "Seeking first the kingdom of God and his righteousness and all these things will be added unto you." Nikki said, "That is a great scripture, one that I will always remember." She gave him his bill and as she handed it to him, he grabbed her hand and kissed the back of it. He said, "I will call you later this evening after class. Okay, you have a good day pretty lady." Nikki said, "You have a good day too, Mr. Bradford."

Nikki cleaned the table and noticed a tip that he left for her that truly put a big smile on her face. She thought, not too bad and took the dirty dishes to the kitchen. Tammy, the hostess cornered Nikki and said, "I saw Bradford kissing your hand. Girl, you got him hook line and sinker." Nikki gave Tammy a smile and a wink and went to the kitchen. Tammy stood there thinking, *it sure is good to see Nikki in good spirits, thanks to Bradford.* Tammy was happy to see Nikki giving her a smile and a wink instead of the evil eye. Tammy was there for her when Nikki lost her son's father in a car accident. She was happy that she was persistent on Nikki to cover Bradford and his friend's table that night.

Nikki started taking care of her other customers and all she could think about was those moist lips that kissed her hand. She worked the rest of her shift and went home. After dinner she headed over to her cousin, Jason's house, they often enjoyed walking together after dinner. Jason was about three years older than Nikki; he had just gotten married and moved a block away from her. His new wife didn't mind because she always had her family at the house. Jason and Nikki would walk and talk about various things when one day Jason asked, "Hey cousin, when are you going to get married?" Nikki said, "I don't know, as they were passing by this big, beautiful church, but whenever I do get married, I want to have my wedding at that church."

Jason laughed and said, "Cousin, you sure do have some big dreams." Nikki said, "Well you asked, and I just answered." They both laughed together and walked home. Nikki asked Jason to come up for a minute because she had something to tell him. Nikki offered Jason a cold drink and told him to have a seat. Nikki brought him a bottle of water and he asked, "What do you have to tell me?" Nikki said, "I met this guy the other night and he and his friend were my customers at work." Jason said, "Well you know, I'm going to have to check him out to see if he's good enough for you." Nikki said, "Yes sir." Nikki and Lois never had brothers and their first male cousins always tried to look out for them, the two sisters. Jason asked Nikki, "Will I be able to meet this person that you met?" "What is his name?' Nikki answered, "His name is Bradford." Jason said, "Before you go anywhere with him, I want his first and last name and his license number, just kidding." Nikki but I do mean business about his first and last name. Jason said, "I just want to make sure my little cousin is going to be all right with this Bradford person."

Nikki walked Jason to the door and told him that whenever Bradford wanted to come over, she would let him know so that he could come and drill him to see what he is made of, Jason said, "Okay!" Just as Nikki was closing the door behind Jason the phone rang, it was Bradford. He said, "I have been calling since about 7:30 p.m., you told me that you got off work at 7:00 p.m. and now it is almost 9:00 p.m." Nikki replied, "Hold up for one minute, let me tell you something, Mr. Bradford. I happened to have a life after work, and I don't have to come home to sit up beside the phone to wait on a call that could very well not come. Now, you called, and I answered, let's talk, but don't ever act like that again!"

Bradford said, "I'm sorry Nikki, I don't know what got into me acting like that. I haven't been myself since I laid eyes on you, let's start over." "Hello, I'm Nikki." "I am Bradford, did you have a good day at work?" "Yes Bradford, I did, what was your day like?"

Bradford told her that he had to take two tests and it felt like his brain was going to explode. Nikki said, "Thanks for the call, Bradford you need to get some rest and relax your brain and you can call me tomorrow sometime." Bradford said, "Wait don't hang up, I want to ask you something." Nikki asked, "What do you want to ask me?" "May I take you on a date?" Bradford asked. "A date?" Nikki asked. He replied, "Yes ma'am a date."

I want to take you to a real nice restaurant and let a waitress or waiter serve you. Nikki paused for a minute saying, "My birthday is Saturday, and I haven't planned anything, you could take me out then." "That'll be wonderful!" Bradford exclaimed. Thank you for letting me be a part of your birthday celebration. "You are very welcome Mr. Bradford, have a good night and sweet dreams." Nikki replied. "Good night to you Nikki and I will have sweet dreams thinking all about you," Bradford chuckled.

WHAT'S IN THE BRIEFCASE?

Nikki hung up the phone. She was so full of excitement and joy that she ran and jumped up and down on her bed. Being home alone, she could really let the kid out inside of her. Nikki was exhausted by all the excitement but couldn't wait to share the news with her big sister, Lois. Nikki called and said, "Sis, guess what?" "What's going on now, it sounds like something really great the way you sound," said Lois. "Girl, it is! I was invited on a date and I'm going to this nice restaurant on my birthday Saturday night!" Nikki exclaimed. "I will get a chance to dress up and you know, I haven't done that in a while."

Lois was very happy for her little sister. "Who will be taking you on a date?" Lois asked. Nikki happily answered, "Bradford, the guy I served at work the other night." "Ok, you know Jason and I will be coming over to meet him when he picks you up. We love you and want to meet the guy that is making you so giddy," said Lois. "I know, because I was going to suggest for you guys to come and give a thorough check of the guy that have swept your little sister off her feet. Jason mentioned that he was going to drill him whenever he came over," Nikki explained. "That's good because I will be doing the same thing," Lois added.

They both shared a laugh together before saying good night. On the other side of town, Bradford was at his apartment walking around saying, "Man, you have yourself a pretty redbone, and the young lady is going out on a date with me! I'm going to show her the best birthday that she has ever had. I'm going to wine and dine her, and she will always want me to be her guy." Bradford had always envisioned meeting that special someone to share his life's journey with.

Bradford was pacing the floor, patting himself on the back before getting into bed. Around 6:00 a.m. the next morning, the phone rang, and it was Bradford. "Sorry pretty lady, I hope I didn't wake you up. I forgot to ask for your address. I thought about it when I woke up," Bradford explained. "Okay," Nikki said, smiling to herself. She gave him the address and he explained, "I will be there to pick you up at 7:00 p.m. I made our reservations at the restaurant for 7:30 p.m." "Okay, that sounds good, but can you stop by my apartment about 6:30 p.m.?" Nikki asked. "Sure," Bradford answered. "I will be there at 6:30 p.m. sharp!"

Bradford didn't know what was going to be take place in those 30 minutes, but he was looking forward to seeing his pretty lady. "Well, I have to go to school now to learn something, talk with you later," said Bradford. "You have a wonderful and glorious day," Nikki answered. "You have a wonderful day, bye-bye," said Bradford. Nikki got out of the bed and went to start her coffee, she decided to call her baby boy and talked with him before he went to school. She dialed the phone number, and her niece Cee Cee answered. Cee Cee always enjoyed helping her mom Lois with Marcus when he stayed with them.

"Good morning niece, are you ready for school today?" Nikki asked. "Yes ma'am," Cee Cee replied. "Let me speak to my baby boy." Nikki added. "Okay, Marcus the telephone is for you," Cee Cee yelled. While he was on his way to the phone, Nikki asked, "Cee Cee was Marcus being a good little guy?" Cee Cee answered, "Well Auntie Nikki," by that time Marcus was pulling the phone from her ear. "I will talk with you later auntie." Marcus said, "Mommy I miss you, when am I coming home?" Nikki replied, "You will be coming home on Sunday, and you will be here for a while because mommy's work schedule has changed. Instead of Uncle taking you to school, you will get a chance to ride the bus from home." "Yay! Yay! Mommy, I love you!" Marcus exclaimed. "I love you too Marcus," expressed Nikki.

By that time, Nikki's brother-in-law told Marcus that it was time to go to school. "Okay Uncle, here I come!" Marcus said, "Bye-bye mommy." Nikki said, "Love you baby boy, have a good day at school and listen to your teacher." "Yes ma'am," Marcus replied. "Give the phone to your Auntie Lois," Mommy said. Nikki was blessed to have Marcus in a very good preschool and was so happy that he was doing well. Lois got on the phone and said, "Good morning, Sis. What are you doing awake this time of morning?" Nikki said, "Bradford called me at 6:00 this morning wanting to know my address and to tell me what time he would be by to pick me up." Lois said, "Good, tell me so that Jason and I can be over there." Nikki told her sister that Bradford would be over at 7:00 p.m. because their reservations is at 7:30 p.m., so I asked him if he could be over at 6:30 p.m. and he said yes." Can you guys get here about 6:00 p.m. or 6:15 p.m.? "Yes!" Lois exclaimed. "Don't forget to bring your keys because I will be getting dressed," Nikki said. "Okay," Lois said, "I will call Jason and tell him that I will meet him at his apartment, and we will just walk over." "Oh yes, I told Marcus he will be coming home on Sunday because my hours have changed, give him lots of kisses from me." Nikki added.

   Nikki loved her sister Lois dearly; she was almost 10 years older than her. Lois always acted like a mother hen to her. Their parents still lived in the Midwest, so Lois made sure that Nikki was always good. Nikki and Lois had a sister that was born in between them but died when she was six months old, the cause of death was Sudden Infant Death Syndrome (SIDS). It is an unexplained death, usually during sleep, of a seemingly healthy baby less than a year old. SIDS is often known as crib death because the infants often die in their cribs. Although the cause is unknown, it appeared that SIDS might be associated with defects in the portion of an infant's brain that controls breathing and arousal from sleep. Nikki and Lois will always keep the memory of their sister in their hearts.

LOOKING GOOD AND FEELING GOOD

Before Nikki started getting ready for work, she sat down to have her morning coffee and put on her detective hat to get a list of the questions that she had on her mind to ask Bradford. She began to write down her questions. What kind of classes are you taking? What was in the briefcase? What kind of job did he have that required him to dress so nicely? Nikki was getting ready to interrogate Bradford on their first date. Bradford didn't know what was in store for him. That was just how Nikki was, always investigating something. She dreamt of going to college and attending law school to become a lawyer, but she became a mom first. Sadly, her dreams were put on the back burner, and they were never visited again. Her parents told her that they would pay for her education but at the time it was not her priority.

Nikki reminisced about hanging out with the wrong crowd, a crowd that did not have any dreams of becoming anything. They only lived for the weekend to hang out and party. By the time Nikki came to her senses, she was older and had the responsibility of raising her child as a single Mom. Not to say that you can't further your education with a child, but it makes it much harder. Due to her choices, she was a full-time waitress and a mom trying to support herself and her son and it was not easy. Nikki was happy that she graduated from high school before Marcus was born.

The day of the date had finally arrived, Nikki woke up from a restless night and couldn't stop thinking about her birthday date night, with her tall, dark, and handsome, God-fearing King that she met on Wednesday night. She could not believe the feeling she was having for this guy. Nikki had just met him a few days ago, not really knowing what he was all about, but he really seemed like a very good catch. It was just something about him that had swept her off her feet and she was enjoying every minute of it. Nikki got up and made her coffee, while it was brewing, she went to her closet to see what outfit she would wear on her first date with Bradford. She had not been anywhere to dress up in a very long time. Nikki loved to shop, and she had a lot of her dress-up clothing that she had never worn. She was so happy to have a reason to wear it now.

Nikki wanted to pick out the perfect outfit to wear, not too dressy but nice and classy. She looked and looked until she came out of the closet with this black pants suit with little white polka dots trimmed in white around the neckline. The buttons were crystal and white and the fabric was soft silk. She couldn't forget about adding the perfect shoes. She pulled out her black patent leather pumps and purse to match. Nikki accessorized her outfit with her pearl studded earrings with a one strain pearl necklace to match. Nikki looked at what she had put together and said if Bradford had been looking at other girls before me, after he saw me tonight, they would be history. Nikki was quite confident in getting Bradford's attention and keeping it. As she was getting dressed, she looked in the mirror and smiled saying, "You go girl!"

Bradford on the other side of town had a restless night. He could not sleep thinking about the young lady he had met on that Wednesday night after Bible study. When she smiled the whole room lit up which made the hair on his head rise. Something about that woman made him feel truly blessed. Bradford heard a knock on the door that morning and it was his friends Tommy Keys and Eddie Bell, they were in college together. "Come on in." Bradford said. "Don't look like you've gotten much sleep last night," Tommy said. "Yes, I tossed and turned all night," Bradford replied. "What's wrong Bradford?" "Well, it's that little, short redbone," Bradford added. Eddie Bell asked, "What redbone?" I forgot to tell you that Bradford met this waitress after we had left church Wednesday night at the restaurant. "She must have been some kind of redbone to keep Bradford from sleeping," Eddie said.

Tommy said, 'Yes, she is a pretty redbone, and if I had not been happily married, I think Bradford and I would be in the running to see who she would choose to be her guy." Eddie added, "I am happily married but I still want to meet the redbone that got my friend not sleeping at night, that he met a few days ago." Bradford chuckled and said, "I just might let you meet her one day. What do you have going on today?" Tommy said, "We stopped by to see if you wanted to hang out with us?" "Sorry guys, I must take the day to chill and get ready for my big date tonight." Bradford said. Tommy and Eddie said at the same time, "Date! With whom?" Bradford had forgotten to tell them that he was going to take Nikki out for her birthday, and he had reservations at this classy restaurant. Tommy and Eddie looked at each other and laughed saying, "Nikki doesn't know it, but she has our friend hook line and sinker." They continued to laugh saying, "All she must do is say jump Bradford and you would ask how high, pretty lady.

"You fellas got jokes. I just want to make a lasting impression on her so she wouldn't mind seeing me again." "We're proud of you Bradford, it is about time you decided to try and settle down." Then Tommy asked, "Have you told her that you were in college for theology instead of art?" Bradford responded, "No, not yet. I don't want to run her off knowing that I will be a minister one day." Eddie exclaimed, "Man, she doesn't know you're going to school to be a preacher?" "Not yet." Bradford explained, "I want her to see me as a man that will make her happy before I tell her. "I do not want you two to say anything until I find the right time to let her know. Do you hear me guys?" Tommy and Eddie responded, "Yes man, we hear you loud and clear." "Bradford our lips are sealed. This is not even our business to be getting into." Eddie agreed, "Man you know us better than that, we are your friends." "Thanks guys," said Bradford.

Tommy started reminiscing about Wednesday night. "I wish you were at the restaurant with us Eddie. You should have seen how Bradford and that waitress was flirting with each other," Tommy added. "Bradford, she just might be the one, the way you are losing sleep and all." Bradford agreed saying, "Yes, and after tonight when I show her how a queen is to be treated, she just may be the one." "Where are you taking her?" Eddie asked. "We're going to that cozy, romantic, Italian restaurant downtown. I heard they have real good Italian food." Bradford explained. "We know where it is but when did you start liking Italian food?" Eddie asked. "We thought you were a meat and potatoes kind of man." Well guys, Nikki said her favorite food was Italian. They looked at each other once again and started laughing, saying Bradford, the Italian food lover. Okay, it's time for you all to go because I have to get ready for my date.

Bradford's friends were very supportive of his newfound love. They reminded him to look his best and get plenty of rest for his date, but wondered why he was getting ready, and it wasn't even 12 o'clock in the afternoon yet. As Bradford was walking them to the door, he laughed and said, "Man it is time for you all to go." Eddie and Tommie laughed letting Bradford know that they loved him and were happy for him. "Thanks guys," said Bradford, he was truly grateful for their friendship. "I will see you all in church tomorrow." Bradford wanted to make a good impression on Nikki, so he went to his closet and pulled out his black and white pinstripe suit, white shirt trimmed in black and starched to perfection, his black and crystal cufflinks and pulled out his black shiny shoes from under the bed.

He patted himself on the back and started his day, waiting until it was time to pick up his pretty lady. Yes, his pretty lady. Bradford had put claims on Nikki to be his wife, but she didn't know it yet. Nikki, on the other side of town was busy cleaning so that Bradford would see that she knew how to keep a house nice and clean and smelling good. Nikki made sure that every dead leaf was pulled from all her plants. She knew that was one of the things a man was looking for in a woman was to keep a clean house. Nikki was always surrounded by wisdom. She would often hear the elders say that cleanliness was next to Godliness.

Marsha, a lady Nikki met years ago, had taken out the time to teach her a few things about becoming a young lady. Lois wasn't in Nikki's life during this time because she had gotten married at a young age and moved away. Marsha taught Nikki that a lady doesn't say ugly words out of her mouth, she should always walk with her head up, shoulders back and tummy tucked. Marsha suggested to Nikki to not have her head up high so that she wouldn't be able to reach down to give a helping hand. She would share a lot of words of wisdom with Nikki. Marsha stressed that whenever you are blessed with a husband you should make sure his house is clean, his food is cooked, his children are clean and fed, and last but not least, make sure you take good care of him in the bedroom, and you will always be treated like a queen. Nikki started remembering how her mother raised her and what Marsha had told her years ago. This was playing in her head as she was making sure everything was in tip top shape from the front door to the back door, every room was spotless. Nikki could hear Marsha saying, *girl you do those things and I'm telling you; you will get all the furs and diamonds that you want.*

Nikki had been cleaning and reminiscing and before she knew it, it was already 4:00 p.m. She went into the bathroom and made herself a hot bubble bath. Then she went to her bedroom to get her undergarments. Nikki laid her black lace panties with matching bra and her black sheer thigh-highs on the bed. Then she went back to the bathroom smiling from ear to ear with so much excitement and hopped in the tub. Bradford decided to call his preacher friend Harry Goodyear. He had already graduated from the Bible College where Bradford was attending. Yes, that's right the college Bradford was attending, and Nikki had no idea that it was a Bible College.

Brother Goodyear picked up the phone and Bradford said, "Hey there my brother, I had a lot of time on my hands and wanted to call and tell you what's been going on with me." "Yes," said Harry. "Tell me what's been going on with you?" "Man, I met this pretty redbone waitress on Wednesday after church," Bradford said. "Tommy and I went to this restaurant to get something to eat. I asked for her phone number, and she gave it to me. I called and asked her for a date, and she told me that I could take her out on her birthday and that was today." Harry said, "Sounds like you really like her." Bradford said, "I sure do, and I just met her and want to know more about her." Harry suggested that Bradford bring Nikki to meet him and his wife Lori. Bradford agreed and said, "That would be great!"

Wow! Harry said, "Sounds like you really like her a lot." "I really do Harry, but it would be a while before I introduce her to you guys," said Bradford. "Why is that?" Harry asked. Bradford told him that she doesn't know that I am in school to be a preacher. I told her I went to the University and was majoring in art. Harry told Bradford don't wait too long to tell her the truth because she will always remember you lied. Bradford changed the subject and told Harry that he was working on this sermon that was good. Bradford and Harry started preacher talk and the time got away from Bradford, when he realized the time had passed fast, it was about 4:00 p.m. He told Harry that he was going to have to go because he was picking his date up at 6:30 p.m. Harry said, "Have fun, I am happy for you." "I'll talk with you later. Thanks man bye-bye." Bradford replied

THE INTERROGATION

Nikki got out of her relaxing, hot bubble bath and wrapped a towel around her and went into her living room to light her scented candles. She went to her bedroom and sat down at her vanity and began to lotion her body with her scented body cream. Nikki started applying her makeup by lining her lips with her red lip liner and putting ruby red lipstick on her lips. She went over to her bed and sat down putting on her black lace panties and bra that matched. Then she started to put on her sheer black thigh highs, started at the toes putting on her left one first and gently pulling it up her caramel brown legs. Next, she put on the right one doing the same thing thinking *if Bradford could see me now,* smiling profusely.

Nikki stood up and went to her full-length mirror and said, *girl you know you are looking sexy, if Bradford was here, he would not be able to keep his hands off you.* From motivation to building your self-esteem, finding joy in the little things helps you concentrate on bringing positivity into your life and shape your feelings and behaviors. Positive affirmations are very beneficial and refreshing ways to bring confidence to your daily self-talk. It also allows you to take control of negative emotions that will decrease stress and harness positive thinking. Nikki came back to reality and said *slowdown girl, slow yourself down, you did just meet this guy.* Nikki started to get dressed when she heard a knock at the door, it was Lois and Jason. She told them to use the key and come on in. Jason and Lois came in the apartment, Nikki stuck her head out of the bedroom door telling them to make themselves at home and get something to drink; she would be out as soon as she finished getting dressed. Nikki went back to her vanity, putting on her sweet-smelling fragrance, spraying it from head to toe, making sure it would intoxicate Bradford's nostrils.

Nikki finished getting dressed and walked into the living room where Jason and Lois were waiting. Jason smirked and said, "She's ready even if she doesn't get a chance to go out." Everyone started laughing. Lois added, "My sister sure does look good and smell good too. Mr. Bradford doesn't know what he is getting himself into, does he?" Jason agreed. "You're right! He definitely doesn't," the two of them laughed hysterically. There was a knock on the door, and it was Bradford. Jason went to the door to let Bradford in, as he introduced himself. "Hey man, I'm Jason, Nikki and Lois's big brother, come on in." By that time, Lois met him halfway saying, "Hello, I'm Lois," Nikki's big sister, "It is nice to finally meet the mystery man that has put a smile on my sister's face."

"Hi, it is nice to meet the two of you," my name is Bradford, but you can call me Brad for short." Nikki will be out in a little bit; she's doing a little last-minute touchup. Jason invited Bradford to have a seat. Jason and Lois didn't hesitate to light into Bradford asking question after question and letting him know to make sure he takes good care of Nikki, while they are out on their date. Shortly after getting grilled from Lois and Jason, Nikki came out of the room and said, "Bradford, I hope my family haven't put the fear of God in you." Bradford took his handkerchief out and started wiping his forehead, saying, "Yes, they sure did." "Well, that's good, now I should not have to worry about leaving the house with you. Nikki added. Bradford thought, *this is a hard-young lady. I don't know if that's good or bad, but I still want to get to know her.* Lois noticed that Bradford and Nikki were dressed in the same colors, black and white. Jason asked Nikki, "Did you guys' plan to be in the same colors?" Nikki answered, "No, but I'm glad we did. Like minds think alike."

Bradford was enjoying the conversation but mentioned to Nikki that they should leave so that they would be on time for their reservation. Nikki went to get her purse and wrap and was ready to go. Lois told Nikki that her wrap was beautiful and asked to borrow it one day. "Sure, my sister, anything for you." The two hugged and Lois wished her a wonderful date night. Nikki said, "You and Jason can stay as long as you want, just lock up behind yourselves and make sure you leave the lights on." "Okay," said Jason, "You guys have fun." Bradford said, "Thanks, and that's exactly what I intend to do for the birthday girl, have a lot of fun." Bradford was a perfect gentleman, he opened the door for Nikki and once they made it to the car, he opened the door for her. Nikki was really impressed by his kindness and truly felt like a queen. The drive to the restaurant was filled with good conversation and nice background music, definitely good music to Nikki's ears.

Nikki told Bradford that she really liked the music. Bradford felt happy that the beginning of the date was going very well. Nikki started pondering in her head all the questions that she wanted to ask Bradford, but just as she was getting ready to say something, Bradford asked, "Do you like to go to the movies?" "Yes, I like the movies. I just haven't been in a while," Nikki explained. "What kind of movies do you like?" Bradford asked. "Well, I like suspense, action and thrillers," Nikki added. "If you're not busy, would you like to go to the movies next weekend?" "We will see, let's just get through our date tonight." Nikki expressed. "Okay, sounds good to me," Bradford agreed.

HAPPY BIRTHDAY FIRST DATE

While Nikki was preparing in her mind to interrogate Bradford with questions, she didn't realize that she had not told Bradford about her baby boy. *Maybe I should invite him over next week for lunch and introduce them that way,* she thought. Just as Nikki was preparing to ask a series of questions to Bradford, they pulled up to the curb at the restaurant for valet parking. The car doors opened, and they were greeted by a nice valet who assisted her with stepping out of the car. Nikki stepped out of the car thinking *this is such a special night on my birthday.* Nikki looked at Bradford and smiled saying under her breath, *now this is the kind of guy I could spend the rest of my life with.* Bradford extended his arm for Nikki to hold on and escorted her into the restaurant.

The hostess asked the name on the reservation, Bradford stated, "Mr. B" then she led them to their table. Bradford had picked a very secluded area in the back corner of the restaurant where the lights were dimmed by candlelight, and a bottle of non-alcoholic bubbly was sitting on the table, the ambiance was breathtaking. Over in the corner, there was a little table sitting off from their dinner table with a dozen red roses, a small gift box and a white teddy bear with a red heart in his hands. The waiter stopped by and said, "You must be the birthday girl! You are in for a treat tonight. This will be a birthday that you will never forget!"

Nikki smiled and said, "Why do you say that?" The waiter added, "Just relax and you will see, because your husband has really gone all out for you on your special day." Nikki didn't correct the waiter when he said husband, she liked the way it sounded. The waiter asked if he could open the bottle of bubbly. Bradford said, "Yes, please." After the waiter filled the glasses, Bradford said, "I would like to make a toast, he stood up and said, "To us Nikki, may we continue to become closer and closer." Nikki said, "Cheers!" She sat there speechless, Bradford explained, "This is just the beginning of a wonderful life that we will share together." Bradford had no idea of the drama that they would soon be in for. The waiter came back to take the dinner orders. Nikki ordered lasagna with a garden salad and Bradford ordered the shrimp platter. The food was delicious, there was a nice atmosphere, and the conversation was absolutely wonderful. They talked about everything; nothing was left for the imagination. Nikki enjoyed talking with Bradford so much that she didn't even think about the interrogation that she had planned.

After the waiter cleared the table, he came back with three more of his co-workers, one was carrying this beautiful small birthday cake with one candle burning. All the waiters started singing the happy birthday song, "Happy birthday to you, happy birthday to you, happy birthday dear Nikki, happy birthday to you!" Nikki blew out the candles and made a wish. She told Bradford, "This is the best birthday I've ever had." She was so thankful for Bradford's kindness towards her. Nikki said, "Thank you so much for making this birthday a special night for me." Bradford said, "You are very welcome, but the night is not over." Nikki smiled and thought, *Bradford surely knows how to make a girl feel special. I wonder what he had coming up next.*

The waiter had an assistant to help him bring the small table that was in the corner to set up beside their table. Bradford gave Nikki the little gift box and said, "Open it up pretty lady." Nikki opened the box, and it was a key. Nikki asked, "What is this key for? Do you have a car waiting outside for me?" Bradford smiled and said, "Well, not yet. This key is for something else." Before she could ask another question, he told her if you would have me, it opens my heart to give all the love I have to you. Nikki stood up and leaned over and gave Bradford a big kiss on the cheek. Nikki shared with Bradford that she would love to accept this key to his heart.

Bradford stood up and they gave each other a hug, Nikki looked up into those sexy eyes and said, "I guess this means that I am your girlfriend." Bradford told her that's right and kissed her on the forehead. Women like to have titles in their relationships. Titles matter if you want an exclusive relationship. It helps to create boundaries and allow you to have a higher level of expectation and commitment. The evening was so special for Nikki's birthday, she hated to see it come to an end. She gathered all of her birthday gifts because it was time to go home. Bradford was very thankful for the superb service that they received and left a big tip in appreciation. He reached to hold Nikki's roses and escorted her to the door. When they got back to the apartment, Bradford helped her carry her gifts in and Nikki asked him if he wanted to stay for a little while. Bradford said, "Okay, but just a little while, then I'm going to have to call it a night." Nikki replied, "Okay handsome."

Nikki told Bradford to sit back and relax, I'll be right back. She went to her bedroom and slipped into something that was black and sheer to match the black lace underwear that she already had on that made her look hot and sexy. There was no way Bradford would be staying for a little while after he got a glimpse of her in her sexy attire. The candles were still burning, she turned off the lights Bradford sat there with his eyes almost about to pop out of his head. Nikki went and sat in his lap. She started kissing him on his cheek and worked her lips over to his mouth, and as soon as their lips touched, the passion was as hot as cayenne peppers. The atmosphere was filled with intense attraction, sexual pursuits, and curiosities. It was hot and steamy. Bradford and Nikki couldn't get enough of each other, their tongues were attached rolling around and around.

Bradford jumped up and said, "I have to go, I hope you had a good birthday, I will call you tomorrow!" Nikki sat there and couldn't believe how abrupt everything had ended, thinking, *that was some hot passion, but it was short-lived.* Nikki said, "Wait Bradford, let me walk you to the door." Nikki asked Bradford if she had done anything wrong, the way he had gotten her off his lap. He kissed her on the forehead and told her, "Pretty lady you've done nothing wrong, it is time for me to leave." Nikki went and sat on the sofa, reminiscing, and thinking, *that guy is full of surprises. I practically threw myself on him and he was a gentleman and didn't even give in to me.* Nikki blew out the candles, got in bed and went to sleep.

Bradford was in his car thanking God that he was able to sustain himself from fornication. He started praying to God to give him the words to tell Nikki that he was a preacher man and to touch her heart so that she would accept him as her guy. Bradford prayed all the way home; he had found a young lady that he wanted to make his wife. He was praying that she would accept him for being a preacher man. He got in bed and fell asleep, still praying as he closed his eyes.

THE TRUTH WILL SET YOU FREE

That Sunday morning, Nikki called Lois and asked if she would have Marcus dressed, because she wanted to go and visit this church that she had seen the other day. Nikki was always visiting different churches, as she had been brought up in church. She was a woman of faith, a God-fearing young lady. Nikki stopped going to church once she got older because she saw so many ungodly actions in the church. Members were holy rollers on Sunday morning but worldly heathens the rest of the week. The one thing that really bothered Nikki was when she would go out dancing on Saturday nights, looking prettier than ever she must add, and dressed for a fashion runway. Later, she would cross paths with their male church pianist, looking almost prettier than her. She was baffled to see him in church Sunday morning playing the piano, with his face red from washing all the makeup off. These situations occurred for a long time. Nikki often wondered why the minister was not going to stop him from playing the piano and he knew the lifestyle that he lived.

Nikki didn't agree with what was going on and decided to stop attending that church. She felt that God was not pleased, and she would never go back there again. Nikki decided to go visit a new church and was going to take Marcus. Bradford went to church often because he was in school to become a preacher man. He went to church every Wednesday and Sunday nights. Bradford was going to have to figure out how he was going to tell Nikki that he was a going to school to become a minister. Nikki and Marcus went to have dinner with Lois and her family. Nikki stayed the whole day at her sister's house and Marcus really had fun with his Mommy. His day was full of activities; after he ate, he was so exhausted that he couldn't wait to go to bed.

Lois always had a house full of food, family, and friends to come over on Sundays. Nikki was telling all of them that she had met her husband. Everyone wanted to know where her new heartthrob was from. They were curious to know more about her mystery man. Some of the family members laughed and said, "Nikki, we never thought it was a man out there to sweep you off your feet." Nikki told them that Bradford was from South Carolina. She added, "He doesn't know how I truly feel about him yet, I am disclosing my feelings for protection and until the time is right."

Nikki told them that her tall, dark, and handsome prince charming had come into the restaurant and had truly placed a mark on her heart. Her niece Cee Cee, her sister Lois's daughter couldn't understand the humor in the conversations about Bradford, because she didn't like the idea of someone coming to take her Auntie Nikki away. Nikki knew that eventually at the right time, she would have to explain to her niece that no matter who she decided to spend her life with, she would continue to love her unconditionally. Nikki fixed her and Marcus a plate to take home. She thanked her sister Lois for the food and told everyone that she had a good time, but all good things had to come to an end. Nikki went to the bedroom to get Marcus up from his nap. She told him it was time to go home. Lois and Cee Cee asked Marcus to come and give them hugs and kisses before he left, they walked them to the car and put him in for Nikki.

When they made it home Marcus went into the den to play. Nikki went into her bedroom to get undressed, then called her parents that still live in the Midwest. Nikki said, "Hello Mother Dear, how are you?" "Tell Dad I said hi." Nikki told her mom that she had met this guy and he was really nice, and he was not a farmer. Nikki always told her mom that she didn't know what kind of man she was going to marry, but she knew that he wasn't going to be a farmer. Nikki always said she got enough of farming when she was growing up, and having no brothers made the work even harder. Nikki hated every minute of farming because she and Lois had to do all the work.

Nikki's mother said, "Nikki Ann, what is the young man's name?" Nikki replied, "His name is Bradford." Nikki Ann was the name her parents called her. Nikki said, "Mother, Bradford is the man I want to be my husband one day." After she said that her mother said, "I hear you, but don't be rushing into marriage, okay baby girl." "Yes ma'am," said Nikki. "Tell Marcus that Grandma and Granddad said hello." Nikki replied, "Yes ma'am, will do. We love you and dad. We'll talk to you later, bye-bye." Nikki called and told Marcus that it was time for his bath so he could get ready for bed because school is in the morning.

Nikki was happy to have her son home. She helped him get dressed, tucked him in bed and read him a bedtime story. She gave him a kiss on the forehead and told him good night. Marcus was excited to be back at home in his bed. He kissed his Mommy and and told her good night. Nikki went to the den to sit down and relax. She started thinking that the next time she and Bradford saw each other, she was going to tell him about her son Marcus. She was in deep thought, *if Bradford is the one, he will have no problem in knowing about Marcus, because if he wants me, he has to accept my son. We are a package deal, and you can't have one without the other.* While Nikki was sitting there the phone ranged, and it was Bradford, sounding rather strange. Nikki asked, "What's wrong?" He told her that he had to talk to her, and he would be over tomorrow afternoon.

Nikki said, "Okay, I will be here waiting for you." Nikki started small talk with Bradford, but he didn't want to talk. He told her that he had an exam to take in the morning and he had to study. She said, "Okay, good luck and have a good night." Bradford replied, "Good night pretty lady." Nikki hung up the phone, *I wonder what's going on with him acting awfully strange. I can't lose any sleep over it.* Morning came so fast it was time to get Marcus up for school. Nikki reminisced about her and Bradford's conversation thinking, *good thing Bradford is visiting in the afternoon instead of the morning because he would have found out about Marcus before I am ready to tell him.* Nikki put Marcus on the bus and went back to her apartment. She thought *since Bradford wanted to talk with her about something important, it would be the perfect time to tell him about Marcus.*

Nikki got her bath and put on some smell good. She slipped on something cute and comfortable that she normally wears to watch her favorite soap opera. While watching TV, she was getting ideas to try on Bradford when he came over. Nikki heard a knock on the door, and it was Bradford. She said, "Just a minute." She rushed and turned the TV off and put on a jazz tape. She was glad she had already seen that episode. Nikki opened the door and there was Bradford, looking as handsome as ever. She grabbed Bradford by his tie and led him to the sofa to sit down. She took his tie off and put it around her neck, and then began to unbutton his shirt, but Bradford grabbed Nikki's hands and told her to stop.

Bradford started buttoning his shirt back up and asked Nikki for his tie back while telling her, "Didn't I say I needed to tell you something that was very important, that's why I was coming over to talk with you." Nikki slumped down back in the sofa with her arms folded, like a spoiled child and said, "Well Bradford start talking." Bradford told Nikki that he meant every word that he had told her on their date and that the key in her gift box was the key to his heart. Bradford added, "When you told me that you would be more than glad to accept the key, those words made me the happiest man on earth. Nikki, it is something that I haven't told you about myself that I really need to get off my chest. Nikki asked, "What is it about you that you're keeping from me?" Bradford started to explain, "Well, you know that I am in college, and it is not the University, it is the Bible College in town." Nikki asked, "Is this the same Bible College that I asked you and your friend about when I first met you?"

Bradford looked at Nikki with sad, puppy dog eyes. Then Nikki asked, "Is there anything else you need to tell me?" Bradford replied, "Yes, there is." "Well, I am waiting, what is it?" Nikki asked. Bradford told Nikki that his major is Theology, not Art. Nikki asked, "So what does that mean Bradford?" "It means that I am a minister and I'm in college to get more knowledge in the Bible so that I will be able to teach and preach the gospel." Nikki looked at Bradford and said, "You are telling me that you are a preacher?" "Yes, that's what I am saying." Nikki jumped up and ran to her bedroom. Bradford sat there not knowing what was going on. He knew that Nikki owned a gun because she lived alone. All kinds of crazy thoughts were going in his head. By the time Bradford decided he might better get up and leave, Nikki walked out of the bedroom wearing an oversized sweatshirt and pair of pants.

Nikki asked, "Where are you going Bradford?" I didn't know what you were doing in there. I know that you have a gun. Nikki laughed and said, "Bradford, I care too much for you to do any harm to you." Nikki told Bradford that she felt so embarrassed for throwing herself at him the way that she had been doing, because she does respect the man of God. Nikki went on to tell Bradford that she was a little upset at him for keeping that part of his life from her. Nikki asked Bradford if he wanted to spend the rest of his life with her. Bradford replied, "Yes, of course I do." Nikki told Bradford I have something to tell you since you want to spend the rest of your life with me. Bradford asked, "What is it, Nikki?" "Well Bradford, I have a little boy and his name is Marcus, he is 4 years old and is in preschool. You will get a chance to meet him that is if you still want to be with me.

Bradford told Nikki, "Girl you got your hooks in me and I am caught like a fish. I want you to be my wife and little Marcus to be my son." Nikki gave Bradford a hug and a kiss on the cheek and told him the story about Marcus's dad. Nikki started talking about Bradford's profession, saying, "I had no idea Bibles were in your briefcase." Nikki told Bradford that they should take things nice and slow, she liked him a lot but didn't know if she was ready for marriage. Bradford had a blank stare with no response. Time was passing by quickly, Nikki told Bradford that she would call him later because it was almost time for Marcus to get home from school, and she was not ready for them to meet. She walked Bradford to the door; he leaned over and gave her a kiss on the forehead. Bradford and Nikki were relieved that they had told each other their secrets that they had been so concerned to share with each other. Now they could move forward to get to know each other better and one day become husband and wife. When Bradford got into his car he sat there for a minute because he'd detected that something was a little different with Nikki after he told her that he was a minister.

After Bradford left, Nikki went and sat on the sofa and said to herself, *I've always prayed for a God fearing, tall, dark, and handsome man with a briefcase.* Nikki always thought he would be a lawyer, a doctor, or a corporate CEO, never in her wildest dreams that he would be a preacher and the briefcase would be full of sermons and Bibles. That day Nikki learned when you pray, you need to be specific in what you're asking for, because she had gotten exactly what she had prayed for, God fearing, tall, dark, and handsome man, with a briefcase full of sermons and Bibles. She didn't ask for a lawyer, a doctor, or a corporate CEO, she just said a briefcase. Nikki wondered; *I'm going to give this a lot of thought before I say yes, to becoming Bradford's wife.* Nikki was waiting for Marcus at the bus stop, he got off the bus and gave his Mommy a big hug. Nikki said, "Let's go down to Auntie Lois's house." Marcus yelled, "Yay!" Marcus loved being at aunt's house, because her two children spoiled him rotten.

Cee Cee and Chester were Lois's oldest; they were the guilty ones that spoiled Marcus. Ryan was Lois's youngest child, and he didn't like the idea that he was no longer the baby in the family, he and Marcus did not get along at all. When they arrived, his cousins were waiting for him in the driveway. They were excited to see him, picking Marcus up and putting him up on their shoulders. Nikki said, "Be careful not to drop him." "I got him, don't worry Auntie Nikki," expressed Cee Cee. Nikki asked them, "Where is my sister?" They said, "She was in her bedroom." Nikki goes in the house straight to Lois's bedroom, closing the door behind her. Lois said, "Hey there sister, how are you doing? I wasn't expecting you down here today, but I'm glad to see you." Lois asked Nikki, "Why did you close the door?" She said, "I have something to tell you and I don't want anyone to hear." Lois was very curious and asked, "Okay, Sis what's going on?" Nikki said, "Sister you would not believe what I found out today."

Bradford came over because he had something important to tell me and he did. Lois asked, "What did he say?" He told me that he is a student at the Bible College and not at the University. He is studying to become a minister and plans to preach at a church one day. Lois said, "Well, that is good Nikki!" Nikki said, "Now I don't know about that Lois, I don't know if I want to be a preacher's wife. I will have to think about this long and hard. I told him about Marcus, and he said that he still wanted me to be his wife and Marcus to be his little son." Lois said, "Nikki that is wonderful, you have a man that loves God, and he wants you and Marcus to be in his life." She told Lois that she was going to think about it and do some serious praying. "Lois, I remember when I was little hearing those mean sisters at the church talking about the preacher's wife and she was very pretty and kind. I don't know if I want to deal with that, especially since we have dealt with people like that all our lives.

Lois suggested that Nikki should bring Bradford over for dinner one day. "Are you guys going to have dinner with us today?" Lois asked. "Yes, because I picked up Marcus from the bus stop and came straight here," Nikki explained. Later that evening they had an amazing dinner, and it was time to go to get ready for work and school. Nikki called out to Marcus telling him that it was time to go home. "Marcus was having so much fun with his cousins, he started crying, asking if he could stay. Please can I stay Mommy?" "Go and ask your Uncle if he would drop you off at preschool in the morning." Marcus ran as fast as he could and then came back and saying, Uncle said, "Yes Mommy, if Cee Cee would get me up and ready in the morning." "Yes, Auntie Nikki, I will get him ready for school in the morning," Cee Cee expressed. "Thank you so much niece, Marcus are you happy now?" "Yes, ma'am!" Well, come over here and give Mommy a kiss good night. Nikki peaked in on her nephews to say good night and to tell Ryan not to bully Marcus. "Yes ma'am, I won't." Ryan said, with a little devilish smile. Nikki said, "Goodnight, love you guys."

Nikki got home and sat on her sofa to relax and started praying to God for direction. She really liked her tall, dark, and handsome preacher man. Nikki felt that Bradford was kind and treated her like a queen, exactly what she had been praying for. Nikki slept very well that night, sleeping until the early afternoon because she worked the evening shift. Nikki lounged around her apartment all day trying not to think about that bombshell she got from Bradford, telling her that he was a preacher. All she was hearing in her head was preacher's wife over, and over and over again. She remembered being a little girl hearing some of those church sisters talking negatively about the preacher's wife. Nikki would always ask her mother why some of the church members were so mean towards the preacher's wife, when she seemed so kind and was very beautiful. Her mother would tell her Nikki Ann, that's how people are when they wish they were you and how people act when they are jealous of you.

While Nikki was reminiscing on how they treated the preacher's wife back then, it made her not want to be a preacher's wife even more. She had already experienced growing up being jealous of and not liked because of who she was. Nikki always liked to dress up and look pretty as a child into adulthood. She knew with her style, self-love, and self-confidence, she would experience the same issues. She was in complete limbo. She had this guy that she had just met, and he told her that he wanted to spend the rest of his life with her and her son. Nikki tried to encourage herself by thinking, *this is what you've been praying for, the man of your dreams, he just happens to be a preacher.*

Nikki engaged in self-talk thinking, *you got just what you prayed for, God-fearing, tall, dark, and handsome with a briefcase full of Bibles and sermons.* Nikki knew that she was not specific in what she wanted in the briefcase, the man of God is who God wanted her to be with. Nikki felt butterflies in her stomach, giddy when she saw Bradford and daydreamed about their life together. There was passion and compassion between the two of them and it wasn't just a physical attraction. With Bradford, they were able to share interesting things with one another. They looked forward to meeting each other's friends and family. There were feelings of excitement, cravings for emotional connection; a long-term relationship that included friendship, family, and a committed partnership. It felt like respect and admiration, safety, and security. There was no lust with Bradford, it was purely love.

SHOP UNTIL YOU DROP

Time had passed quickly. Nikki rushed to get ready for work. When she got to work, the dinner rush had started, and it was very busy. Nikki worked three hours straight, her tables stayed full, and her pockets were being filled with tips. After the rush was over, she suggested to Tammy since her station was slow, she would go ahead and take her break, Tammy agreed. Nikki took her break, she made herself a salad, got something to drink and went straight to the break room. Once she sat down, she slipped off her shoes to relax and catch her breath. Nikki thanked God for her food and begin to eat her salad. As she was eating, she started to think about the conversation she had with Bradford.

Her imagination started to run wild. She was full, relaxed and thinking about Bradford. Tammy came to the break room and said, "Nikki your break time is over, you have three customers in your station. I've already given them water, silverware, and a menu." "I will tell the three young men that you will be to their table shortly." Tammy added. Nikki thanked Tammy, she slipped her shoes on and headed out to take care of her customers. Nikki was happy and thanked God it was not Bradford and his friends because Tammy said three gentlemen, and Bradford usually brings his friend Tommy Keys. Nikki put on her smiling face and went to take her customers' orders.

When she walked up to her station there were three customers waiting to get their orders taken, but to her surprise it was two of her customers, one was Bradford, Tommy Keys, and another guy that she hadn't seen before. They all went to the Bible College together. Nikki said, "Hi my name is Nikki, are you guys ready to order?" They said, "Hi," in unison with big smiles on their faces. Bradford seemed a little shy, because he wasn't sure how to respond because of what Nikki had said the last time he saw her. The third guy said, "Hi Nikki, my name is Eddie Bell, and I am friends with Bradford and Tommy Keys. I had them to bring me in this evening because I just had to meet this young lady that Bradford can't seem to stop talking about. Now I can see for myself you are all that Bradford have been telling me."

Eddie Bell went on and on, then Bradford said, "Alright Eddie that is enough. I am sure Nikki got the message from you about how I feel about her." Nikki said, "Nice to meet you Mr. Eddie." "Are you guys ready to order?" Tommy Keys said, "Yes, I am, but first, I would like to give you, my congratulations." Nikki asked, "Now Mr. Tommy Keys, what on earth are you congratulating me for?" "Well, Bradford told us that he had proposed to you. Nikki replied, "So, did he also tell you that I never said yes." Tommy Keys said, "Well, I just believe it's just a matter of time." Tommy was going on and on while Nikki was giving Bradford the evil eye. His friends had no idea that he was sitting in the hot seat. They didn't know that Nikki had told Bradford that she wasn't ready to get married. She didn't like that Bradford had shared some of their private conversations with his friends. Bradford told his friends to go on and place their orders. After they placed their orders, Nikki tended to the window to inform the cooks that the orders were placed. She went straight to the break room so she could count to 10, because she was so angry at Bradford. He was acting like they never had a conversation the night before.

Nikki mentioned to him that she would get back in touch with him when she had time to process him being a preacher and becoming his wife. Nikki went to Tammy and asked if she could leave early and to give her customers to one of the other waitresses. Tammy told Nikki that she would make sure that her customers were taken care of. "Get your things and have a good night," Tammy said. Nikki told Tammy, "Thank you so much for being such an understanding hostess." On her way home, Nikki wondered if Bradford was the one that would make a good life for her and her son Marcus. Nikki didn't know what to do. She had always prayed for a good, God-fearing man, tall, dark, and handsome with a briefcase, she had never given any thought to ask for certain things to be in the briefcase. She had not ever dreamed that there would be

Bibles. She thought about how Marcus was growing up so fast and needed a father figure in his life. Bradford assured Nikki that he would take good care of her and Marcus.

Nikki could not stop thinking about the life she had always dreamt about, the fairytale life with a handsome guy that would come and sweep her off her feet. She visualized him being financially stable to meet all of her and Marcus's needs and wants. Nikki was not sure if Bradford was the guy, she still needed time to think. It seemed like their courtship was moving way too fast. Nikki went to pick up Cee Cee to come and have a sleepover with her. Nikki left Marcus with his cousins, Lois two boys. Cee Cee just loved spending time with her Auntie Nikki, staying over to her house, made her feel like a big sister. Nikki told Cee Cee that they would go out to dinner and catch a movie, because the next morning they would be cleaning the apartment. Cee Cee was so excited! She said, with a big smile on her face, "Yes ma'am!"

They gave each other a hug and were ready to enjoy their quality time together. Nikki and her niece Cee Cee had a blast of fun that evening. When they returned home, they were ready to get in bed, but before turning in for the night, Cee Cee gave her Auntie Nikki a big hug, telling her thank you for a super night. "I love you," Cee Cee said. "I love you too sweetie. Sweet dreams and good night," replied Nikki. The next morning Nikki got up and fixed Cee Cee her favorite breakfast, bacon, and eggs with blueberry pancakes. Nikki was making sure she spoiled her niece the whole weekend because she was very helpful with taking care of Marcus.

Cee Cee was loving every minute being spoiled by her Auntie Nikki. It was about 12:00 p.m. and there was a knock at the door. Surprisingly, it was Bradford. Cee Cee was mad because she didn't like the idea that it was a man in her Auntie Nikki's life that could possibly take her away from her. Cee Cee let him in giving him the evil eye saying, "Auntie Nikki, this man wants to see you. He is in the living room; I think it is that man you call Bradford." Nikki came out of the bedroom and said, "Hello Bradford, I didn't expect to see you." Bradford asked Nikki if she could please step outside to talk. Nikki told Cee Cee to start getting dressed because they were going to the mall and shop until they dropped. Cee Cee loved hearing those words because she loved to shop, just like her Auntie Nikki. Cee Cee had forgotten all about Mr. Bradford at that moment.

Just as she was walking away to start getting ready, Bradford said, "So you are Cee Cee," as he gave her some money to buy her something nice, "I hope you have a lot of fun with your Auntie." Cee Cee smiled and said, "Thank you, Mr. Bradford." She walked to the bedroom to get dressed. Once Cee Cee made it to the bedroom, she looked at the money saying to herself, *this is only $20 he could have at least given me $50 since he is trying to take my Auntie Nikki away from me. Well, I guess $20 is okay, he didn't have to give me anything.* She humbled herself and remained grateful.

Nikki went outside and asked, "What is it, Bradford?" "Girl, I can't hardly function in my everyday life not knowing what's going on with you. I know you said that you needed time to think but this waiting is killing me." Bradford exclaimed. "I was going to call you on Monday to come over and meet Marcus," Nikki explained. Suddenly a big smile came on his face showing that big gap in the middle of his pretty white teeth. Nikki asked Bradford to come over about 4:00 p.m. and asked him to be hungry, because she had prepared a feast. "I'm going to cook dinner for you so you can see that I do know how to cook." She added.

"You have truly made me a happy man, Nikki," Bradford expressed. "If the Lord says the same, I will be here Monday at 4:00 p.m." He leaned over and gave Nikki a kiss on the forehead. By that time, Cee Cee was looking out the window and got a glimpse of Bradford. Thinking out loud, *you better keep your lips to yourself.* Nikki went back into the house calling out to Cee Cee, asking, "Are you about ready to go?" "Not yet, Auntie Nikki." A few minutes later Cee Cee came out of the room looking sad. Nikki walked over to her putting her arms around her.

She asked. "What's wrong sweetie, why are you looking so sad?" "Are you going to marry that man Mr. Bradford, Auntie

Nikki?" Cee Cee asked. "Well, Auntie doesn't know that right now, but he did ask me to marry him. If I did decide to say, "I Do," then you would have a really tall uncle." Nikki tried to make Cee Cee feel a little better knowing that she wasn't fond of Bradford. Nikki looked into her eyes and explained to her, "Cee Cee, no matter who comes into my life, you will always be my big girl and gave her a big hug. Come on and let's go get dressed so we can do what we love to do, shop!" Nikki knew exactly what to say to make her niece happy and put a big smile on her face. Cee Cee still felt that Mr. Bradford was trying to take her Auntie away from her. Cee Cee and Nikki enjoyed their quality time together. Nikki knew that her niece needed some tender loving care from her and some retail therapy. They were shocked at how quickly the weekend had passed by. It was Monday morning and Nikki started getting Marcus ready for school. Nikki told him that she had a guest coming over for dinner and she wanted him to be a good little guy. She wanted him to be on his best behavior. Marcus was very well-mannered, and she knew that he would make a good impression for Bradford. Nikki told Marcus that her friend Mr. Bradford was coming to visit, and she was excited for the two of them to meet. Marcus smiled.

GUESS WHO'S COMING TO DINNER?

As Nikki was walking to the bus stop, she told Marcus that she really liked Mr. Bradford. "I will be a good little guy Mommy," said Marcus. "Thank you, my handsome little son," Mommy said. Marcus told his Mommy, "You're welcome," as he gave her a tight hug and hopped on the bus. Nikki walked back to the apartment overflowing with joy. She sat down at the kitchen table and began preparing her menu for dinner. She started daydreaming about the unexpected Saturday morning visit from Bradford, reminiscing about him leaning over and kissing her forehead with his hot, sexy lips that touched her hands. The moistness felt so good to her that she had to pinch herself, then she thought, *girl he is a preacher* then quickly bounced back to reality. Nikki got back focused and finished writing the menu. She later went to the grocery store to buy what she needed for the special dinner for her son and the preacher man.

Bradford on the other side of town was getting ready for class, trying not to be excited about the dinner he would be going to later that evening. It was hard for him because that redbone Nikki got him right where she wanted him, and he didn't even care. Bradford tried to think of something to make a good impression, so he decided to take Nikki a bouquet of flowers. Next, he thought about her son. Bradford started to think about what he liked to play with when he was a little boy. He wanted to put a smile on her son's face, so he thought a sports car would make the perfect gift for him. He decided to go shopping after he finished with classes.

Lois called Nikki just as she was bringing in the last grocery bag. She scurried to the phone just in time to say hello. Lois asked, "Nikki why are you out of breath?" Nikki explained, "I had to run up the stairs to get to the phone. I will call you back in about 15 minutes, then I will explain what is going on, nothing serious though." Lois responded. "Ok, call me back in 15 minutes." Nikki put the food in the refrigerator, then called her sister Lois back. Nikki told Lois that she had invited Bradford over for dinner, so that she could let Marcus and him meet. Lois said, "I sure would like to be a fly on the wall this evening," then she laughed because she knew how Marcus could act up when it comes to a man liking his Mommy.

Nikki mentioned to Lois that she had already told Marcus about the dinner and her friend coming over before he went to school. "He said he would be on his best behavior," Nikki added. Lois said, "Lil sis, I will believe that about Marcus after the dinner when you tell me how everything went." They both laughed. "I will talk with you later so that you can start preparing your dinner. Good luck and I will talk with you later," said Lois. Nikki went into the kitchen and started preparing dinner. She thought about the conversation between her and her sister and what she said about Marcus, hoping that he doesn't misbehave because she knew her son.

It was 3 o'clock, one hour before dinner and 30 minutes before Marcus got home. Nikki went in for a quick shower and put on a cute sundress that made her peanut butter complexion glow. She looked in the mirror thinking, *when Bradford sees me, he's going to want to be the jelly to my peanut butter*. Nikki looked at the clock, it was time to go and get Marcus at the bus stop. The bus was pulling up just as she was walking across the street. Marcus jumped off the bus, gave her a big hug and kiss on the way home. She asked, "Did you have a good day in school?" He said, "Yes ma'am, I had fun, and I learned a whole lot." Nikki told Marcus as they were going into the apartment to be a good little guy today, because my friend is coming over for dinner. Nikki asked Marcus to tell her about what he had learned at school while preparing dinner.

Nikki was so proud of Marcus and how well he was learning new things in school. After they discussed his day at school, Nikki mentioned to Marcus that he had changing clothes on his bed to change for dinner. Nikki told Marcus to put on his changing clothes, then put his dirty clothes in the hamper and not on the floor. Although Marcus was young, he understood that his Mommy wanted him to be nice to this man that she seemed to like. Marcus started thinking, *I will have to see what kind of man he is before I will be nice*. Marcus had been the man of the house for so long, he was not going to let just anyone come into him and his Mommy's life.

Suddenly, Nikki called out to Marcus. "What are you doing in there daydreaming?" She asked. Marcus had a little grin with his hand hiding his face. Nikki didn't know what he was thinking but could tell that his imagination was miles away. A few minutes later Marcus came out of his room with a nice blue jean playset on. Nikki told him how handsome he looked; he was smiling from ear to ear. That made him feel really good. Nikki admired how Bradford seemed to be a man of his word. She never had to guess what he was thinking because he was very vocal about his feelings for her. He pulled up and before coming inside the apartment he could smell the food aroma through his car windows.

Bradford got out of the car and in one hand he had a vase full of beautiful colorful flowers and in the other hand a gift bag with two shiny sports cars inside for Marcus. There was a knock on the door and Nikki told Marcus, he's here. Nikki opened the door and there stood this tall, dark, and handsome man. Nikki just wanted to melt the way he had just made her feel, just seeing him standing there. Nikki said, "Come in Bradford. How are you doing this evening?" "Just fine now, that I'm here with you guys," Bradford said. Then he said, "These beautiful flowers are for you." Nikki told him thank you and reached for the flowers telling him that she would make these their centerpiece for dinner. Bradford said, "This bag is for Marcus." Nikki was so happy that Bradford was so thoughtful to bring her and Marcus a gift. Marcus was watching TV, she asked him to come over and meet Mr. Bradford.

"Yes, ma'am," said Marcus. Bradford was really impressed to hear this little guy say, "Yes ma'am" to his Mommy. Nikki told Marcus, "This is my friend, Mr. Bradford, Mr. Bradford, this is my son," said Nikki. After introducing the two guys, Bradford and

Marcus shook hands, both saying, "It is nice to meet you." Bradford politely passed the gift bag to Marcus, telling him this is for you. "Thank you," Mr. Bradford," Marcus said. "You are welcome little fellow. It is so nice to meet you. I sure hope you like what is in the bag." Marcus went back to sit by the TV and looked in his bag, he pulled out two shiny sports cars and his little face lit up like it was Christmas morning.

He jumped to the floor and ran over and gave Mr. Bradford a hug around his legs, because he was so tall. Bradford reached down to pick up Marcus saying, "Wow! I guess you really like the cars." Marcus replied, "Yes sir, thank you!" Bradford was very happy that he could put a smile on Marcus's face. Nikki glanced at them from the kitchen feeling good that the two of them were hitting it off. Nikki called out from the kitchen telling the guys that it was time to wash up for dinner. Marcus grabbed Bradford's hand and led him to the bathroom. Marcus got on his stool, turned the water on, and started to wash his hands. He jumped down from his stool and got a paper towel and dried his hands. "It's your turn now, Mr. Bradford," Marcus expressed. He started washing his hands.

Bradford thought to himself, *Marcus is such a smart, little guy.* By the time Bradford had finished washing his hands, Marcus was holding a paper towel for him to dry his hands. They both walked out together and headed towards the kitchen. Nikki was already sitting at the table. Marcus walked and sat in his chair. Nikki asked Bradford to give thanks for the food. After Bradford blessed the food, it was Marcus' turn to bless the food. Marcus begins saying his prayer, "God is good. God is great, let us thank him for our food. In Jesus name. Amen."

Bradford shouted, "Good job, good job Marcus!" Marcus felt good getting compliments from Bradford, his smile was as bright as the sun. Nikki got Marcus a plate and went to the stove to fix his food, then she told Bradford that dinner was being served buffet style. Bradford got up to fix his plate and said, "Nikki, you have really outdone yourself!" He told her that it had been a long time since he had a home-cooked meal with a variety of food to choose from, thank you so much for inviting me.

Nikki told Bradford to help himself and eat as much as he liked. "You will be taking a to-go plate home to have for your dinner tomorrow," she added. "Oh wow, thank you so much," Bradford replied. Everyone started eating. Marcus said, "Mommy this food is so good!" Bradford agreed with him, "Yes, it is good!" After dinner Nikki sent the guys to the living room while she was cleaning the kitchen and putting the food away. That's when she realized that she had forgotten about dessert. Nikki went into the living room and asked Bradford if he could watch Marcus while she went to the store. He said, "Yes," then he looked at Marcus and asked, "You don't mind me watching you, do you little buddy? We could play with your new cars." Marcus said, "Yes, that sounds like fun!"

While Nikki was gone Bradford and Marcus were playing with the new cars and talking like they had known each other forever. They were sitting there talking and having fun and just out of nowhere Marcus asked Bradford, "Are you going to marry my mommy and be my daddy?" Bradford looked at Marcus trying to gather himself to answer this question that this little guy just asked, while at the same time, wondering how this little guy came up with a question like that. Bradford went over and sat on the sofa and asked Marcus to come and sit beside him so that they could have a man-to-man talk.

Bradford explained to Marcus that he would marry his Mommy tomorrow if she said yes, and he would absolutely love to be his Daddy, then he gave Marcus a big hug. Nikki walked in the back door with dessert. "Hey guys, what did I miss?" She asked. Nikki saw the guys hugging so she ran over and jumped on the sofa. I want some hugs too! She expressed. All three of them gave each other a big hug, laughing hysterically. Then Bradford and Marcus turned on Nikki and started tickling her. She laughed and tried to get away. She was finally able to get free and ran to the kitchen asking them if they wanted milk with their chocolate Chester cookies. "I would like milk Mommy," Marcus replied. Nikki said, "Okay son," then Marcus asked Bradford, "Would you like some milk?" Bradford answered, "I sure would like some milk with my cookies. You can't have chocolate Chester cookies without milk."

While Bradford was answering, they made quick eye contact with each other. They both had to say a quick prayer to themselves to keep their fleshly desires controlled. Bradford was still sitting beside Marcus but quickly got up and went to the bathroom to get himself together and stay focused. Bradford loved Nikki and Marcus. He wanted to make sure he wasn't lusting after the woman that he wanted to marry. Nikki watched as Bradford got up to go to the bathroom, thinking *that man is so handsome.* She had to pray about her lustful thoughts and keep her mind together remembering that Bradford was a preacher man.

	Nikki made a tray with cookies and milk and brought it into the living room. They sat there just like one big happy family watching TV, drinking milk, and eating chocolate Chester cookies. Bradford told Nikki that he could get use to enjoying quality time together. Nikki agreed, "Yes, maybe one day I would like that for us. I'm just not ready yet." While Nikki was letting Bradford know how she felt, Marcus said, "Mommy I'm tired, can I take my bath in the morning?" "That'll be fine son. Go and get your pajamas that are under your pillow and put them on and then come and tell Mr. Bradford good night." Bradford told Nikki that Marcus is mature for his age. "Yes, he just amazes me sometimes with the things that he says," said Nikki. "I can truly contest to that." Bradford remembering what the little guy had just asked him while Nikki was gone to the store.

	Marcus came back to the living room to let his Mommy know that he was ready for bed. He walked over to the sofa and said "Nice to meet you, Mr. Bradford. Have a good night." He extended his hand to shake Bradford's hand. Bradford extended his hand back and shook Marcus's hand. Bradford said, "Nice to meet you, young man and I hope to see more of you. Have a good night's rest." Nikki took Marcus by the hand and told Bradford the remote was on the coffee table and that she would be out in about 10 minutes. When I tuck Marcus in, I read him a bedtime story every night. "Wow!" Bradford said. "You're such a good mother taking very good care of your son."

While Nikki was in the room reading Marcus a bedtime story and tucking him in, Bradford was sitting on the sofa thanking God for letting him meet Nikki the waitress, his future wife. Nikki gave Marcus a kiss on the forehead, pulled the blankets up and told him to have a good night's rest and thanked him for being on his best behavior. Nikki went back to the living room with Bradford. Bradford told Nikki that he really had a good time and was thanking her for the invitation to meet her son, and the good home cooked dinner. Then he thanked her for a wonderful and glorious evening. Nikki told him that she enjoyed the evening too and was glad that he was able to come meet her son, eat dinner and watch a movie together. Nikki asked Bradford to sit back and relax. Bradford exclaimed, "No, I will be leaving now, as he was standing up from the sofa."

In a very disappointing voice, Nikki said, "Ok, let me walk you to the door." She was not ready for him to leave. Nikki had planned to cuddle with him on the sofa, with her legs overlapping his, holding his cheeks and kissing his lips, but that was not going to happen that night. They walked to the door, Bradford gave Nikki a kiss on the forehead and said, "Good night beautiful." Nikki replied, "Good night handsome" and closed the door.

BIBLE STUDY BLESSINGS

Once Bradford got in the car, he held the steering wheel thanking God that his flesh didn't get weak. He was happy that he didn't give in to temptation and lust. Nikki looked out the window and watch Bradford as he pulled off, in disbelief saying, "Wow, he wants to marry me!" Nikki walked to the bathroom to run herself a hot bath. She relaxed in the tub thinking how she wanted to kiss Bradford's lips. Nikki quickly had to shake that way of thinking because he was a preacher man and she started having lustful, fleshly thoughts. Nikki got in bed and tossed and turned until she fell asleep. Bradford was at his apartment doing the same thing, tossing, and turning until he finally fell asleep. He went to class the next morning, and as soon as he pulled into the parking lot Eddie and Tommy were standing there waiting to find out all about his dinner with Nikki and her son.

Bradford got out of the car with a big smile on his face, making his friends even more curious. They asked, "How did it go yesterday?" "Everything was great!" Bradford exclaimed. "We can tell everything went great by the look on your face, but we would like to have detailed information." "Would you like for us to just ask the questions or are you going to volunteer the information?" Eddie and Tommy asked. Bradford said, "Hold up brethren, I don't mind you asking your questions, but you do know when it's time for class I will be going to class and not answering your questions. Do you understand that?" They agreed. "Yes, we do." "Did the little boy like you?" Yes, the young man and I connected very well. He seemed to like me a lot and we had interesting conversations for him to be so young. Bradford explained.

Bradford quickly went straight to talking about her cooking like he was reading his friend's mind. "Yes, Eddie she can cook," Bradford added. "Yes, man she really can throw down in the kitchen.

Her food was good and well-seasoned, just right, exactly like I like it." Tommy asked again, "So, did her son seem to really like you?" "Yes, he did." Bradford answered. After dinner, Nikki had to run to the store for milk and cookies and you would not believe what that little man asked me. "What?" They asked in unison. "If I was going to marry his Mommy and be his Daddy?" "Well, what did you say?" Tommy and Eddie asked. "Guys, I didn't know what to say at first, I had to gather my thoughts and remember who I was talking to and how old he was." Eddie asked, "What did you tell him?" "I told him the truth, that I would ask her to marry me in a heartbeat. If she said yes today, I would marry her today." Bradford explained. "How did he react?" Eddie asked. "He just smiled." Bradford added.

"Sounds like her little son is a smart, cool little guy." Eddie said. Bradford bragged at how intelligent Marcus was to be so little. He told his friends, "I would love to be that little guy's Daddy." Bradford said, "Tommy, if you don't mind, I want you to have a Bible study with Nikki." "Okay, Bradford, let me set it up and I will let you know." Tommy said. It was time for class, Bradford and his friends went on to class. Nikki put Marcus on the bus and told him that she would see him in the morning. She reminded him that his Uncle would pick him up from school and he would stay at Auntie Lois and Uncle's house tonight with his cousins. Nikki called Lois and told her that Marcus and Bradford got along good. Marcus didn't even get mad about anything; he acted just like a perfect little gentleman. Bradford really enjoyed the home-cooked meal too. Lois was happy that everything went well. Nikki told her sister that she had some errands to run before she got ready for work. "I will talk with you later. Oh, and thank you all for always helping me with Marcus." Nikki expressed. "You are very welcome," Lois said.

Nikki started her day taking care of some business before work. She got to work, and the girls saw her come in the door and started saying, "Look at Nikki's glow. I believe love is in the air." Nikki said, "Maybe it is or maybe it's not, I would never tell." They laughed and said, "Girl whatever, we can look at you and tell for ourselves." They laughed and got ready to work the dinner rush, this was the busiest time for the restaurant. After Bradford finished classes, he and his friends Eddie and Tommy went over to

Bradford's apartment. "Can you finish telling us about last night with Nikki and her son?" Eddie asked. Bradford was still thinking about that hot passionate kiss that he wanted to give her but was happy he was able to stay focused. He wanted to tell his friends about it, but he was not sure how they would handle it, so he kept it to himself. Bradford's imagination took off into another world. I think I will keep that to myself.

Tommy and Eddie said, "Hey man, where were you in La La land earth to Bradford, earth to Bradford." Tommy and Eddie said, "Man, you're not going to get out of telling us about your dinner with Nikki and her son." "Well, last night was magical. It was everything I had hoped for and more." Bradford explained. "Last night must've been something else since you went into that deep thought after we questioned you." Tommy said. "It was a wonderful evening with Nikki and her son Marcus. Dinner was delicious and it was just like we were one big happy family sitting together watching a movie after dinner." Bradford thoroughly explained. Tommy and Eddie looked at Bradford and said, "Wow man, we are so happy for you. It sounds to me that you have been bitten by the love bug," Eddie said. Tommy said, "I agree my friend, sounds like you are in love and that's a good thing, you have a wife and a son." Tommy and Eddie had worked up a big appetite after asking Bradford all those questions about his dinner date. They headed to the kitchen asking him what he had to snack on. Bradford told them to check in the kitchen pantry and refrigerator. After a few snacks and more conversation about Bradford's dinner date, the guys left and headed home to their families.

Nikki got home from work and there was a message from Bradford asking her to call him. She called him before she took off her work clothes. The phone rang and Bradford answered. Nikki greeted him by saying, "Hello handsome." Bradford responded by saying, "Hello beautiful." Nikki asked if it was something special, he wanted to talk about, other than to hear her voice. He said, "Yes, I want to talk to you." "May I come over, if it is not too late?" Bradford asked. She said, "No, come on over." "Alright, I'll be there in about 15 or 20 minutes," Bradford confirmed. Nikki said, "I will be waiting."

Bradford was so glad she told him that it was not too late to come over. After Nikki got off the phone, she ran to her bedroom and got out of her work clothes and jumped in the shower. While she was drying off, she had a thought to just keep the towel on that was wrapped around her and when she opens the door to let Bradford in and drop the towel on the floor. Nikki laughed and thought *you better not do that, because he may turn around and run back to his car.* Nikki did not know what to put on, everything she thought of that night would turn Bradford around at the door. She put on a long T-shirt and some leggings, two pieces of clothing should be just fine with just a little dab here and there of her smell good.

Nikki heard a knock at the door and immediately started smiling, thinking he's here. She went to the door to let him in glancing at herself as she passed the long mirror in the hallway, giving herself a wink. "Come in Bradford and have a seat. Would you like something to drink?" Nikki asked. "Anything is fine with me," Bradford said as he sat there watching Nikki walk to the kitchen with her long-fitted T-shirt and leggings, remembering what had first attracted him to her. All Bradford could think about was Nikki's butt looking like it was breathing when she walked. Bradford sat there very still lusting after Nikki as she walked into the kitchen wearing her long-fitted T-shirt. Her outfit was making him see a lot more than he could when she had on her waitress uniform. He had to quickly call on the Holy Ghost because his flesh had started to lust. Nikki walked in with his soda, holding the glass coming out of the kitchen, while Bradford secretly enjoyed the scenery, staring at her shapely frame silently saying, *sit on me Holy Ghost.*

Nikki said, "Here's your soda Bradford." He was so glad to have a soda to cool him down. He took a big gulp of his soda trying to get his mind back focused. Nikki made it real hard for him to focus, looking as good as she was in her lounging clothes. She sat down on the sofa beside Bradford. He asked, "Have you thought about what I asked you?" "Yes, I am still thinking about what you have asked me and how it is going to change the rest of my life. I want to be sure when I give you the answer." I also stopped by to tell you that Tommy would like to have a Bible study with you. He wanted me to check with you to see when you're available. "A Bible study?" Nikki asked. "What do I need a Bible study for?" Bradford answered. "So, we will be members of the same church when we get married." Nikki said, "Hold up Bradford, I haven't said yes yet." He said, "You will one day soon," looking at her with his starry eyes, raising his eyebrows up and down. Bradford's eyes made Nikki want to melt all over the floor. She was truly seasick in love with him. He knew that he had sexy eyes, that's why he was doing that, Nikki thought. She remembered his eyes were one of the things about him that had attracted her to him.

Bradford said, "Earth to Nikki, earth to Nikki." She laughed and said, "You see what will instantly put me in a trance." Nikki was back focused and was ready to get back on a serious note. Nikki told Bradford there are some things that I want once I become your wife. Bradford said, "Ok, let's hear it!" Nikki began requesting a loving family with a nice home, with a beautiful fireplace, nice cars, diamonds, and furs. I want Marcus to have the best education that money can buy. "No problem, I will be able to give you a good life and provide for you," explained Bradford. "I can do some of that now. While I'm in school I can keep a little money in your pocket but when I get out of Bible College and get a church then I can do all those things you asked of me."

Nikki agreed to have a Bible study, but she admitted that she still was not ready to say yes to his proposal. If Bradford had only known the church folks they were going to meet, and the upcoming events they would have to endure, he would not have made those promises. Nikki asked Bradford, "Why can't you give me a Bible study?" Bradford answered. "I am too close, and I want you to be my wife. I don't know if I would be able to stay focused on teaching the Bible to you, about the plan of salvation, that's why. I'm not going to conduct the study." "Ok, I understand," Nikki said, putting her hand on his leg giving a little squeeze. He patted her hand and moved it saying, "Well Nikki, I guess I will be on my way home." You don't have to leave; Marcus is at my sister's house. Although it is hard, Bradford stayed focused, and said, "Yes, it is time for me to go." "Ok, then." Nikki stood on top of the table and said, "Give me a big, good night hug." He said, "Okay." As she was hugging his neck, she gave his ear a little nibble. Bradford shook his head. She pulled away and said, "Give me a good night kiss." Nikki pulled his face to hers and laid a big, long kiss on him. Before he could catch himself, his hands were on her butt gripping it tightly.

Bradford shook the lust off and told Nikki that they needed to stop. She said, "No, I won't," so Bradford had to be like Joseph, he ran leaving his coat behind. Nikki said, "Bradford wait!" I will call you tomorrow, running to get into his car. Once he got in his car, he took his hand and wiped his face, saying, "Thank you Lord for getting me out of there before we had gone too far, before our marriage to each other." Nikki went and sat back on the sofa feeling bad about coming on to Bradford, like she didn't know he was in school to become a preacher. She didn't know what had come over her. The lusting was at an all-time high! She truly felt bad about what she had done. When he got home, she was going to call him and apologize for her behavior. Nikki had given Bradford time to get home, then she called him. "Hey there handsome. I just wanted to apologize for my behavior tonight. Sweet dreams and good night." Nikki hung up the phone before Bradford could say a word.

The next morning Marcus called asking if he could stay with his Aunt Lois and Uncle for the rest of the week. Nikki asked Lois if it was okay. Lois said that the children enjoyed having him there. Nikki said, "I'm sure Marcus really wants to stay because you all spoil him rotten. I will call him later to say good night." Nikki asked, "Hey Lois, why don't you and my brother-in-law have another child? That way your children will have a little brother or sister to play with." "I don't think that they would like that because then they could not send them home when they got tired of them," said Lois. Nikki laughed and asked, "Oh, is that why they enjoy Marcus so much?" Lois laughed and said, "Yes, that's about right." Lois asked, "How are you and Bradford getting along." "Pretty good, I'm going to have a Bible study with him and his friend Tommy Keys." Lois asked, "Is that Bible study going to get you ready to be a preacher's wife?" "I was kind of thinking the same thing when he asked me about having a Bible study. Bradford said it was to learn the plan of salvation so that we will attend the same church after we get married," Nikki explained.

Lois yelled, "Sister, you didn't tell me you had told him yes!" "No, I haven't yet, I am trying to take my time, but I want to be sure of this lifestyle commitment," Nikki explained. "Yes, make sure you are ready because sometimes I wonder about your brother-in-law," Lois said. "What do you mean Lois?" Nikki asked. "I just wonder about things sometimes, that's all," Lois added. "It was nice chatting with you this morning, have a good day, I must start my wifely duties. Goodbye." Nikki didn't have to be at work until 2:00 p.m. Marcus was not home; and she was excited about her free time. *What am I going to do with myself with all this time on my hands?* She thought. Perhaps I will call Jason this evening, we haven't been walking in a while. I will get dressed and treat myself to some pancakes and sausage with coffee. Afterwards, I will walk my breakfast down by going to the mall and shop, shop until I drop. Nikki started to drift away daydreaming, thinking *hopefully she and Bradford would get married, and he would make that big money and she wouldn't have to work.*

Nikki had been thinking long and hard about becoming a preacher's wife. She loved to shop and buy herself very nice things. She loved to buy hundred-dollar shoes for only $15-$25. Nikki always seemed to be able to find the nicest things on a budget that would be a plus for Bradford, if she ever decided to say yes. She stayed gone all day. When she got home Bradford was pulling up just as she was taking the bags out of the car. Nikki was happy, thinking perfect timing, he will see what I like to do in my spare time. Nikki greeted Bradford, "Hi baby, you're just in time to help me take these bags to my apartment." "I see you have been grocery shopping," he said, "Well, I've been shopping but not for groceries." She laughed. "No, these are shoes, dresses, pants, blouses, and a couple pieces of jewelry. I had all this time today, so I just went shopping and had a ball." Nikki explained. Bradford laughed and said, "It looks like you had more than a ball." After they put the bags in the room, Bradford sat down in the living room. Nikki sat next to him and confessed that she loved to spend money. "I work hard and definitely play hard." She explained.

If I get married, I am still going to spend money and work only if I want to, not because I will have to. Bradford said, "Nikki what have I been telling you if you marry me and be my wife, I will keep you happy. I will make the money and you will be able to go on a shopping spree. Just trust me Nikki, I love you and I will provide for you and Marcus." She said okay, "I will see, and I will make sure you are not forgetting what you are telling me." "You can tell Tommy Keys that I will have a Bible study with him. You can let him know I will be off work tomorrow and you guys can come over after you finish classes. Please call me in the morning to let me know." Bradford was so happy to hear those words come out of Nikki's mouth, thanking God silently that she was ready for the Bible study. There was a knock on the back door, Bradford could not see who it was, all he knew that it was a man's voice.

Nikki and Jason walked in the living room, Jason said, "Hey, how are you doing man, I haven't seen you since I met you that night you took little sis out for her birthday." Bradford answered, "I'm doing good man, thanks for asking." "It seems like to me just looking at the two of you, love is in the air, and I am happy for you guys," Jason said. "Nikki, did you still want to go walking?" Jason asked. "Yes," Nikki said, "I went shopping today and found so many good deals and I am just getting home, but I still would like to go before it gets dark." "Ok." Jason said, "I will come back after dinner." Bradford told Jason looked like she bought out the store. Jason explained, "That's my little Sis, and she loves to spend money. When is the big day?" Bradford told Jason that she hadn't said yes yet. "When she does decide, he would be one of the first people she would tell."

"Ok, I'm going to hold you to that." Jason said. "I am going home and have dinner with my family and will give you a call later." "Tell the family I said hello," Nikki said. "Will do," expressed Jason. Nikki asked Bradford, "What are you getting ready to do?" "I'm getting ready to go home." He replied. "Please take me with you, because I don't have anything to do, and I want to see where you live. "Ok," Bradford said. Then he thought to himself, *I sure hope she keeps her hands off me when we get to my apartment. Lord, please let her keep her hands to herself.* Bradford silently prayed. Nikki said, "Let me get my purse and keys and I'll be ready to go. They pulled up to the apartment, and it was in a nice neighborhood.

As they entered the apartment, Nikki was looking all around. Bradford had it looking nice and clean to be a single man. It had a small living room, and the kitchen was combined, the bedroom, closet, and bathroom were also combined.

Nikki's thoughts were, *if I marry him, we sure won't be staying here. We would have to find something a little bigger when he is finished with school, and we are joined with a church.* After she finished taking a tour of Bradford's apartment. He asked, "What do you think?" You have it fixed up nicely, but it is very small. As Nikki started to sit down on the sofa, Bradford came and sat down beside her. "I'm glad you like it." He said. Nikki reiterated, "Yes, but it is just so small." Nikki suggested if she said yes to Bradford's proposal, then they would need a house or bigger apartment than what he had. Bradford agreed. Nikki asked, "When would you like to start looking? What about before your Bible class tomorrow?" She asked. "I will be finished with all my classes before noon." Bradford replied. "Ok, great!" Nikki expressed. "Sounds like a plan." Nikki asked Bradford to let Tommy Keys know what time they will be back to her apartment after house hunting tomorrow, so that he may be able to stop by. Bradford called Tommy Keys and told him that Nikki was ready for the Bible study. He told Bradford to tell her that he was unavailable tomorrow, but he was free right now.

Bradford said, "Well, she's here with me now, let me ask." Bradford explained the situation to Nikki, Tommy was happy that she agreed to have the Bible study. "I will be over there shortly," said Tommy. Tommy asked, Bradford, do you have an extra Bible?" Bradford replied, "Man you must have forgotten who you're talking to." "Oh sorry, I forgot," Tommy said. Nikki asked Bradford if she could use his telephone, back then cell phones were unheard of but could come in handy. Bradford was curious to know who she was calling, but he said yes. Nikki dialed the number, and the phone ranged. Jason picked up and said "Hello." Nikki said, "Hey there big brother, just calling to let you know I'm not going to be able to walk with you this evening." As always, Jason was very understanding and said, "Okay no problem, you two lovebirds have a good time." Nikki said, "Okay."

As soon as Nikki got off the phone, Bradford was standing there saying, "Woman, I didn't know who you were calling on the phone." She slowly turned as she was hanging the phone up, giving Bradford an unpleasing look. He knew he had said or done something that she didn't like. "What's wrong sweetheart?" Bradford asked. Nikki expressed, "The statement you just made." "What statement?" Bradford asked. "The one that makes it seem like I have to tell you every single time where I'm going or who I'm talking to." Nikki explained.

Nikki said, "I will not marry or live with someone that I have to get permission to talk on the phone, or to go where I want. When I marry, I will be totally committed to my husband only and he would not ever have to wonder about my loyalty." Nikki added, "Bradford, if I decide to say yes to your marriage proposal you will have a faithful wife for life." Once Bradford saw Nikki was very serious, he said sweetheart, "I always want to show you how much I care for you and how I want you to be my wife for life. Please forgive me for my actions, with being so overprotective of you, that's something I am really going to have to work on, because I do not want those kinds of actions toward you to run you off." Bradford leaned over and put his arms around Nikki and gave her a kiss on the forehead.

He stood up from the sofa and asked Nikki if she would like something to drink or eat. She asked for something to drink and sat back down getting comfortable on the sofa waiting for Tommy Keys to show up for Bible study. While waiting, Nikki started thinking *what kind of Bible study she was getting ready to have with Tommy Keys.* She had gone to church almost all of her life, so she just sat there wondering and waiting. Nikki heard Bradford in the kitchen making noise with pots and pans. She knew she had smelled something very delicious when she walked in the door. Bradford had put a meal in a crockpot before he went to class that morning. All he had to do to complete dinner was put the rolls in the oven. Nikki hollered in the kitchen saying to Bradford, "I smell something smelling good, is it done yet?" He told her as soon as the rolls brown, you are more than welcome to eat dinner with me. Nikki said, "Yes, thank you, I would love to have dinner with you. Now, I will be able to see if you can cook since you want me to be your wife. I need to know if I have a husband that can cook." Bradford answered "Yes, I know how to cook, my mom and five sisters made sure of that." Bradford added, "If Tommy comes before we are finished eating, I will offer him some dinner too." "That's so nice of you to offer your friend something to eat," Nikki said. Bradford and Nikki were able to finish their dinner before Tommy came over. They cleaned the kitchen together and sat down on the sofa and waited on Tommy.

NIKKI'S WATER BAPTISM

There was a knock on the door, it was Tommy Keys. Bradford invited him in. Nikki stood up and said, "Hi Tommy." Then Bradford said, "You guys can come to the kitchen table." They all sat down, Tommy asked Nikki a few questions. He opened the Bible and started teaching the plan of salvation. He asked, "Nikki, do you believe Jesus Christ is the Son of God?" She answered, "Yes!" Then he asked, "Are you ready to get baptized for the remission of your sins?" She answered, "Yes!" Bradford stood up and reached to pull Nikki up, then gave her a big hug. Tommy called his preacher friend that happened to be the minister of the church. Tommy asked Minister Madden if he could use the baptistery because he had just finished a Bible study.

Tommy's preacher friend told him to meet him at the church and he would have everything ready. When Tommy got off the phone, he had a big smile on his face. "Nikki, are you ready?" Tommy asked. "Yes, I am," Nikki said. They all got their belongings and went and got in the car and headed to the church. When they pulled up at the church, Nikki asked, "Is this the church where I will be baptized?" Tommy answered, "Yes, it is." Nikki was quite surprised, she told them that this was the church that she would always tell her big cousin Jason that she was going to get married at. "Now tonight I will be baptized here, how about that!" Nikki expressed.

They went in on the side of the church when they saw the preacher and two young ladies. He said, "Hello, I brought my daughters to help the young lady get ready for her baptism." Bradford, was very grateful, saying, "Thank you my brother." The young ladies introduced themselves to Nikki and asked if she would follow them so they can help her get ready for her baptism. Nikki had no idea of the details of the baptism, but she knew it would be a life-changing experience for her and Bradford. Minister Madden asked, "Who will be baptizing the young lady?" Bradford replied, "I will be doing the baptizing." The preacher said, "Will you follow me so I may show you where to get dressed." Bradford got dressed and went to the water. The young ladies helped Nikki up the stairs, then Bradford helped her into the water. Bradford reassuring her that everything is going to be fine, then he baptized her dipping her into the water, saying "I baptize you in the name of the Father, of the Son, and of the Holy Spirit."

When Nikki came up out of the water, she was so happy that all her sins had been washed away. Nikki went back to the dressing room all wet looking for the young ladies to thank them for helping her, then she gave them a big hug. Bradford took Nikki by the hand and said, "Welcome to the Christian family Sister Nikki." "Thank you, Bradford," then Nikki pulled Bradford to her and asked him if he would ask the preacher if they could have their wedding ceremony at his church. Bradford said "Yes, I sure will right now." Bradford walked over and asked, "Minister Madden, I would like to ask you something?" He responded, "Sure what is it? He asked. Bradford shared that Nikki, his wife to be, would like to have their wedding ceremony here at your church. He responded, "Yes, of course you can, just let me know as soon as you set a date, so I can put it on the church calendar." Tommy confirmed that he would be conducting the ceremony for them.

Tommy, Bradford, and Nikki thanked Minister Madden for letting them use the pool at his church and Nikki thanked him for letting her and Bradford have their wedding ceremony at the church. They went back to Bradford's apartment. Tommy said, "I hate to run but the family should be home by now." Bradford and Nikki got out of the car and the two of them thanked Tommy for all he had done for them on that evening. They went into the apartment holding hands. Bradford opened the door and Nikki went straight to the sofa and sat down. "Baby, lock the door and come sit down beside me," Nikki expressed.

Nikki told Bradford that they should start looking for a larger place, so when they did get married, they wouldn't feel cramped up. Bradford agreed. While sitting watching TV, a romantic movie just happened to be on. Nikki put her hand on Bradford's knee, he jumped straight up and said, "Nikki, it is time to take you home." She laughed saying, "Wow! Bradford, all I did was touch your knee." Bradford started to explain, "Yes, I know, that's why I'm taking you home. Come on let's go." Bradford drove Nikki home; he walked her to the door and gave her a kiss on the forehead and said good night.

Nikki went to her apartment and sat down on her bed and started crying. She was not crying because she was sad, she was crying tears of joy that all her sins have been washed away. She thanked God for letting her be one of his children. She got ready for bed and slept like a baby. The next morning Nikki started praying to God asking him to give her direction in her life because she wanted to marry Bradford one day, but she was afraid of commitment. Nikki continued to pray. Nikki decided that she wouldn't worry but instead leave the matter of marriage in God's hands. Nikki got up and started her day. She was really missing Marcus so she called Lois and told her she would be down there later that day to see her little prince. Nikki told Lois to let Marcus know that he had one more night to stay, then he was coming home. Lois said, "Okay, I will surely let him know."

Lois could tell in her sister's voice that something was wrong. "What's wrong Nikki? "Oh, nothing?" Nikki answered. Lois said, "Girl, I helped mother raise you and I know when there is something wrong with you." Nikki explained, "Well, I guess you could say something is wrong." "Ok, what did he do?" Nikki asked, "What did who do?" "That Bradford fellow." Lois added. Nikki said, "No, he didn't do anything wrong." What is it that has you troubled? Lois asked. Nikki answered, "Bradford is still asking me to marry him, that's what's wrong. Nikki added. "I have good news, last night I got baptized after having Bible study with Tommy Keys. Bradford dipped me in the water, baptizing me for the remission of my sins and I was added to the body of Christ."

"Lois, I am overjoyed about being a Christian!" Nikki explained to Lois that she wanted to marry Bradford, but she didn't know if she was ready right now. He is always asking and now his friend has started asking right along with him. Nikki asked Lois, "Don't you remember how they talked about the preacher's wife growing up? We used to ask Mama why they are so mean and hateful towards the first lady. Well, it will be me that they will be talking about, and I will have to deal with church folks the rest of my life. I want to be very sure of my decision because I only want to say I do until death do us part only once." Lois said, "Little sister you have given me an ear full." Nikki laughed and said, "Well you did ask what was wrong, so I just told you." "Little sister that is all in your hands, you are the one that is going to have to make that decision," Lois explained. Nikki told Lois that she had been praying about it and she wanted to know how Marcus felt about Bradford becoming his Daddy.

Nikki thanked her sister for having a listening ear and always giving her great advice. I'm going to clean my house, run a few errands, and I will be down to your house later. "Lois, I love you, have a good day. See you later." Nikki said. After getting off of the phone with her sister, Nikki laid around before she started cleaning her house. While she was lounging on her sofa, she reminisced on things she had asked God for. She had always wanted a husband with a briefcase, tall, dark, and handsome with a profession that would take care of her and her son and make it possible for her to be a stay-at-home Mommy, allowing her to hire a maid if she wanted to. She thought maybe her prayers were coming true.

THE GREATEST GIFT FOR MARCUS

Nikki never thought that the God-fearing man with the briefcase, would be a preacher in Bible College living off his G.I. Bill from the Army, wanting to marry her, and she wanting to marry him. She had already mentioned to him what she wanted once she said, "I do." All Nikki kept hearing was Bradford telling her we would have money once I finish school and become a Pastor. Nikki was thinking about the church she grew up in, remembering how well the preacher and his family was taken care of. Nikki still remained indecisive on the topic of marriage until she and Marcus had a family meeting.

Nikki got up, cleaned her house, and ran her errands. She came home, got dressed and went to her sister's house to see Marcus. Nikki always had a lot of fun visiting her family, having dinner, and seeing her son. She explained to Marcus that he would stay at Auntie Lois's house tonight; Uncle would take him to school in the morning and she would pick him up from the bus stop after school tomorrow. Nikki was very thankful for her family's support. She gave Marcus a hug and kiss and told him she loved him. Nikki told Lois that dinner was delicious and thanked her again and the rest of the family for helping her take care of Marcus.

On Nikki's way home, all she could think about was the answer she was going to give Bradford. She wasn't ready to rush into a marriage that might not work out. She had been raised by her parents always telling her, "one wife for life," and "one husband for life," that's why she wanted to be very sure before she accepted his proposal. The next day, Nikki went to get Marcus from the bus stop. She asked him if he had a good day in school, he replied, "Yes ma'am." They went up the stairs to the apartment and Nikki told

Marcus that they were going to have a family meeting. She told him to come sit down because it was something important that they had to talk about. Marcus sat at the table, like a big boy waiting for his Mommy to tell him what the meeting was about. Nikki asked, "Marcus, do you remember Mr. Bradford that came over for dinner?" He said, "Yes ma'am." "Well, he wants to marry me and be your daddy forever and ever."

Marcus smiled and said, "Mommy, I asked him if he was going to marry my Mommy?" Nikki was in complete shock. She asked, "Marcus, who told you to ask him that?" Marcus explained, "Nobody, it just came in my head Mommy." "Well, what did Mr. Bradford say when you asked him that?" Marcus added, "Mr. Bradford said, "Yes! I want to marry your Mommy that is if you let me little man." Nikki asked, "What do you think about Mr. Bradford being your daddy? How would you like that?" Marcus said, "Yes ma'am, he could be my daddy since my real daddy died."

Nikki told Marcus, "God has blessed us with a daddy that loves God, so he will love us. Nikki and Marcus gave each other a hug, then she told him that she would give Mr. Bradford a call and have him come over and give him an answer to his proposal. Marcus started jumping for joy because he never had a chance to call anyone daddy, because his daddy had gotten killed before his mommy even knew she was going to have a baby.

Nikki called and asked Bradford to come over when he had a chance. Bradford told her as soon as I put on my shoes, I will be over. Nikki couldn't believe it, Bradford seemed to arrive in a blink of an eye! Bradford thought, *it was always a pleasure to be in the company of Nikki.* She opened the door and let him in, when suddenly Marcus ran and jumped in his arms and gave him a big hug. "Come in and have a seat, I would like to talk to you," Nikki said. Marcus went into the bedroom to play. Nikki addressed Bradford, "You have been asking me if I would be your wife and grow old with you, well Marcus and I had a meeting and we decided, "Yes! We would like you to become a part of our family. Yes Bradford, I will be your wife!" Bradford was the happiest man alive.

He had been waiting and praying to hear those sweet words from Nikki. God had truly answered his prayers.

Nikki started making her request to have a big church wedding. "I will make sure you get that, but we will have to wait one year after I graduate. We can have it on the same day of my graduation." Bradford said. "Are we going to be engaged for one year?" Nikki asked. Bradford suggested that they go to the Justice of the Peace and let the judge marry them. Nikki responded, "I know the perfect day that we can get married." "What day would that be?" Bradford asked. Nikki explained, "Marcus's birthday, and we'll be getting married exactly 90 days after we met." "That's a wonderful idea!" Bradford expressed. They were happy that God had put them together.

Nikki had to get things together for her son's birthday party at school. She suggested to Bradford that the three of them could go to the courthouse after Marcus's birthday party was over. Then Nikki reminded Bradford about the church wedding she wanted at the church where she had been baptized. "I haven't forgotten. We will need to tell the Pastor of the church ahead of time when we set a date for our wedding." Nikki wanted to make sure that Bradford didn't forget about her dream church wedding. "Let's call Marcus in and let him know that we will be getting married on his birthday," Nikki said. Bradford said, "Let me go into the bedroom to get him and will walk out together, my son and I." Nikki's insides were gleaming with excitement. She will soon have two handsome men in her life. Bradford and Marcus came in the living room and sat down on the sofa with Nikki. Bradford told Marcus; we have good news to tell you. His eyes opened wide, excited to hear the good news. Nikki said, "Marcus, Mr. Bradford will become your daddy on your birthday." Marcus was so excited he knew his birthday was coming up soon and now he would have someone to call daddy.

Nikki told Marcus he would be putting on his tuxedo next year when they have the big church wedding, which is also the same day that Bradford will be graduating from Bible College. Marcus gave Bradford a hug and said, "I love you daddy." Bradford silently got emotional, appearing to shed tears, hearing Marcus say those words. Bradford said, "Let's go out and celebrate!" Bradford asked Marcus, "Where do you want to go?" Marcus yelled, "Chucky Cheese!" The three went out, played games, ate pizza and had so much fun at Chucky Cheese. The next day Nikki got Marcus ready for school and walked half a block from their apartment to the bus stop. She told him that they would come to the school after they ate lunch, to talk with his teacher to make sure it was okay to have a birthday party in his classroom. Nikki enjoyed volunteering as a parent helper when she was off work. His teacher always liked it when she would come to visit. Nikki wished Marcus a good day at school, gave him a hug and put him on the bus. She went back to the apartment and got dressed because she had a few stops to make before she went to visit Marcus's teacher.

Just as she was getting ready to leave the telephone ranged, it was Bradford. He was calling to confirm the exact time to pick her up to go and see Marcus's teacher. Nikki responded, "11 o'clock would be fine." Bradford asked, "Why are you rushing me off the phone?" She explained that she had a lot to do before he picked her up. As Nikki returned back home while putting away everything that she had bought for the birthday party, Bradford knocked on the door. Nikki thought, *he is handsome and prompt because it was 11 o'clock sharp.*

They went to the school to see Marcus's teacher, Mrs. Lancaster and asked if they could bring his birthday party to school on tomorrow, after they had lunch. She said, "Of course, that would be just fine." Nikki asked, "After the party would it be okay for Marcus to leave with us?" Nikki was so excited; she told his teacher that they wanted to take Marcus with them because they were going to the Justice of the Peace to get married on Marcus's birthday. Mrs. Lancaster was so happy for Marcus and his mom to be getting a daddy and a husband tomorrow.

NEW BEGINNINGS OF LOVE

Bradford and Nikki thanked Mrs. Lancaster and gave Marcus a hug and told him they would be at the bus stop waiting for him after school. The next day they went to Marcus's classroom with balloons, party favors, cake, and ice cream. Mrs. Lancaster mentioned how Marcus had been nothing but a little chatterbox all morning and during lunch. He was so excited about his birthday party and getting a daddy after his birthday party was over. Bradford smiled with delight and so did Nikki. Mrs. Lancaster congratulated Bradford and Nikki on their upcoming marriage. The birthday party had started, Marcus and his preschool classmates had so much fun playing games, dancing, singing songs and eating cake and ice cream.

Bradford and Nikki cleaned up the classroom. Marcus was happy to celebrate with his teacher and peers, especially being showered with a few birthday gifts. As they prepared to leave, everyone gave Marcus a hug and told him that they would see him tomorrow in class. Bradford, Marcus, and Nikki headed to the car, Marcus asked, "Mommy, are you going to get married now?" She answered, "Yes baby boy, and gave him a kiss on the cheek." The three of them were on their way to the courthouse. Nikki said to Bradford, "I'm having butterflies in my stomach." Bradford said, "I feel the same way, it is happening to me too." Nikki added, "We must be doing the right thing." Bradford agreed and said, "Yes Nikki, we are doing the right thing, because the Bible says it is better to marry than to burn with passion."

Nikki continues to need reassurance asking Bradford, "Are you going to be good to me and Marcus?" He replied, "Yes woman, I want you to be my wife and Marcus my son. I'm so glad I met you and while we are at the courthouse, I am going to find out what I need to do to adopt Marcus, so that we will be one happy family."

"You will be the Queen in our home, Nikki." Bradford added. Those words brought tears to Nikki eyes as she told him that he will be the King in their home. By that time, they were pulling into the parking lot of the courthouse. Nikki told Bradford, "My butterflies in my stomach are gone." Bradford agreed saying, "Mine are gone too!" They got out of the car and held Marcus's hands, walking together to the courthouse with their son in the middle to become an official family. Bradford told the front desk clerk that they were there to get married. The clerk replied, "Congratulations! Go down the hall and make a right and they will be able to help you." When they arrived, the desk clerk asked, "Are you here to get married?" Bradford and Nikki replied in unison, "Yes." Suddenly, with a loud voice Marcus shouted, "Yes!" Everyone laughed.

The clerk asked them to have a seat and fill out the paperwork. After reviewing the papers, she saw that Bradford's mother and Nikki's mother had the same maiden name and asked if they were related. "No, if we were related, we would not be here to get married," Bradford explained. They both gave her a look that made her apologize for asking such a question. She looked over the paperwork and asked them to follow her to the judge's chambers. When they walked in, it was the judge and two witnesses. Nikki started thinking, *I am here getting ready to marry this man that I met only 90 days ago, in a room with a judge, two people that I don't even know, and my son.*

Nikki started to have second thoughts about what was getting ready to happen. Before she had a chance to think a little more, one of the witnesses started asking if they were ready. Bradford said, "Yes!" Nikki was still in deep thought, Bradford had to touch her to bring her mind back to reality. The judge pronounced them husband and wife and told Bradford, "You may kiss your bride." Bradford leaned down and kissed his wife with a gentle, passionate kiss. Nikki put her arms around his neck and the judge cleared his throat. Marcus was pulling on Nikki's arm because they had forgotten where they were with their long kiss.

Bradford apologized to the judge and thanked him for marrying them. Bradford and Nikki were husband and wife; the three of them walked out of the judge's chambers one happy family. As they were leaving Bradford asked the receptionist where he would need to go to inquire about adoption. She verified the process of what he would need to do. He thanked her and told Nikki let's go check it out. Nikki suggested for them to come back another day. Bradford asked, "Why not now?" She explained that Lois was at home waiting for them. "Oh yeah, that's right!" Bradford quickly remembered. "Did you forgot she's going to keep Marcus so that we can have a weekend honeymoon?" Nikki asked. He was still adamant about getting those papers for the adoption, so they quickly followed the receptionist instructions and got exactly what they needed. As they pulled up in Lois's driveway, there were all of these cars and a lot of people. They didn't know what had happened. Nikki's heart started pounding, she feared the worst. She thought something had happened to one of her family members. Bradford, Nikki, and Marcus got out of the car and walked to the house, everyone started blowing bubbles and throwing rice and saying, "Congratulations!" It was a pleasant surprise for the newlywed couple. Nikki and Bradford were overjoyed with the love and support they had from their family and friends.

Lois, Jason, Tommy Keys, Eddie Bell, and their wives had set up the wonderful, surprise wedding reception for Bradford and Nikki. It was very nice with a lot of people from the Bible College and many family members. Bradford and Nikki got a lot of wedding gifts and many guests decided to give Marcus gifts too. They enjoyed themselves, eating good food, fellowshipping with family and friends, cutting the wedding cake, and taking lots of pictures. It was a wonderful day of celebration! The newlyweds were truly ready to start their honeymoon. They had decided to spend the honeymoon at Bradford's apartment. Nikki had made it so romantic that when Bradford carried her across the threshold, the passion was so hot that the clothes started flying all over the apartment. Bradford and Nikki had become one and the marriage was consummated in the eyesight of God, they were no more two but one.

IN SICKNESS AND IN HEALTH

Bradford was about to find out early in the marriage about sickness and in health. Nikki had a dentist appointment the next day after they had gotten married. Bradford had one class and they were going to meet for lunch. When Nikki got to the restaurant, her mouth was still numb from the filling she had gotten that morning. The newlyweds really enjoyed their lunch. Bradford and Nikki finished lunch and went home to get their special dessert. When they woke up from their nap, Nikki was in excruciating pain from the filling she had gotten that morning from the dentist, the numbness was no longer there, and she was in tears. Bradford did not know what to do at first, he just took his new wife in his arms to comfort her the best way he knew how to do.

Bradford placed Nikki's head on the pillow and told her he would be back. Bradford called the dental office to tell them what had happened. Unfortunately, the office had closed early so he called the dentist emergency phone number. He explained to the dentist what had happened to his wife on their honeymoon. The dentist was very empathetic and called the pharmacy to order some pain pills for Nikki, in order for her to have some relief. The dentist advised Bradford to have her in his office first thing Monday morning. Bradford thanked the dentist and told him that they would be there bright and early. Bradford went into the bedroom, Nikki was crying like a little girl, she was in so much pain. Bradford kissed her on the cheek and told her that he was going to the pharmacy to get her some pain pills, all she could do was nod her head in agreement.

Bradford drove to the pharmacy; he thought about the wedding vows they had shared on yesterday in sickness and in health. Well, Bradford was surely getting to see what those wedding vows meant only one day after he said them. Bradford got back with medicine; Nikki was still crying. He got her a glass of water and gave her a pain pill, then he took his shoes off and sat in bed and rocked his wife until the pain medication had knocked her out. Bradford sat there and watched his new wife, although she was asleep, she looked as beautiful as ever. He sat there thanking God for his beautiful wife, the gift that he had been blessed with. He was happy and very relieved that she was not crying anymore and in no more pain. The next morning the first thing Nikki did was get a pain pill. She went back in the room and Bradford was sound asleep. Nikki thought to herself, *I guess I took Bradford through something last night, being a big baby, but he really did take good care of me.* Nikki said, "Thank you Lord for my husband you gave me." She showered, put on her honeymoon clothing, went to the kitchen, and cooked breakfast for her husband. Nikki put it on a tray, then she went to the bedroom and gave Bradford a washcloth and told him to sit up in bed because she had a surprise for him. As he was waking up his eyes opened really wide, seeing his wife walking away, wiping his face so he could see more clearly. He thought to himself, *she has me hooked like a fish.*

She said, "Here's your breakfast my King," and then she thanked him for taking really good care of her on last night when she was acting like a big baby. Bradford told her, "You are my big baby Sweetheart." Nikki put on some soft music while Bradford enjoyed his breakfast. She modeled for him because she had something special for him after he finished. Bradford got excited; he still had a plate of food when he mentions to her that he was finished with his breakfast. Nikki laughed and suggested that he go on and eat because he will need his energy. Bradford laughed but agreed to eat his food while he sat and enjoyed her modeling. Once Bradford finished his breakfast, Nikki asked, "Honey, did he get enough to eat?" Bradford replied, "Yes sweetheart, I am full, everything was delicious and thank you for the live entertainment." They both laughed and caressed each other. The passion was in full effect.

Bradford and Nikki honeymooned all day and night. When they woke up it was Sunday morning, time to get ready for church. Marcus was going to church in the country with Nikki's family, they would see him after church. The newlyweds headed to church, but Nikki started to experience butterflies because this was going to be her first-time meeting Bradford's church family. She was sure they were going to be looking at her. Nikki loved dressing up with everything matching from head to toe, with all the right accessories to match. As a little girl she always liked to play dress-up. Nikki was praying that the church members would not prejudge her before they got the opportunity to get to know her. In Nikki's past, people have looked at her outer appearance and concluded that she had an attitude problem. Nikki was nothing like that, she just liked to dress up. Thankfully, her smile was what let the members know that she was a true child of God. The church that they attended was the church that was connected to the Bible College Bradford was attending.

After church, Nikki and Bradford went to the country to her sister Lois's house to have dinner and pick up Marcus. Lois had a house filled with cousins and friends. Everyone was eating, laughing, and talking, having a good time. Jason, Nikki's cousin said to the newlyweds, "You guys sure do look tired." Then another cousin asked, "I wonder why?" Her cousins all started laughing. Jason added, "We know why, you guys been honeymooning!" Bradford smiled and Nikki agreed and said, "You know that's right, we have been honeymooning because we are married now!"

Marcus was standing right beside Bradford and Nikki, he asked, "What is a honeymoon?" Bradford explained it to Marcus saying, "A honeymoon is when a man and woman gets married and they go away to be alone, just like me and your mommy did on Friday, when we left you here with your auntie, uncle, and cousins, that's a honeymoon son." Lois smiled and said, "You sure did fix that answer up just right for Marcus." They all laughed. It was time to go. Bradford had a good time getting to know Nikki's family and friends at her sister's house. Nikki asked, "Cee Cee, would you go and help Marcus get his things together?" "Yes ma'am," Cee Cee replied. Lois called Nikki in the kitchen to fix some dinner plates to take home with them. Nikki asked Bradford to come in the kitchen to fix what he wanted on his plate, and she fixed hers and Marcus's plate.

Nikki insisted that Bradford get enough food for tomorrow's dinner. The newlyweds were getting ready to leave, telling everyone what a good time they had and thanked Lois and her family for taking care of Marcus. Cee Cee walked out of the bedroom with Marcus with his things and everyone in the house walked out saying their goodbyes to Bradford, Nikki, and Marcus, the first family headed home. Once they made it home to Nikki's apartment, they started getting ready to start the week, Marcus getting ready for school, and Bradford to Bible College. Before he went to class that afternoon, he took Nikki to the dentist to find out what was going on with her teeth. She had gotten a filling, but she was still in so much pain that Monday morning.

After the dentist took care of Nikki, Bradford took out his handkerchief and wiped his forehead, thanking God for letting him get through Nikki's pain as her new husband. The dentist told Nikki that the medicine he was prescribing to her, she would have to be off work for the rest of the week. She said, "Okay and asked if he would call her job and let them know." Nikki was still floating around from the pain pills she had taken before leaving home. Bradford helped his wife to the car and headed home. He took Nikki to the bedroom so that she could lay down, he called the college to let them know he would not make it to class today or tomorrow because he had to take care of his new wife that was sick.

Once Bradford got off the phone, he went into the kitchen to see what he could cook for dinner, he opened the freezer and was overwhelmed seeing all of his choices. Nikki had all kinds of food to choose from, Bradford thinking out loud, *Nikki being my wife, I would never have to worry about having enough to eat.* Bradford entered the bedroom and asked Nikki if she wanted some lunch. She told him no she would wait and eat dinner when Marcus got home from school, then slowly went back to sleep.

Bradford took food out of the freezer so he could cook dinner later, then he went to the car and brought his briefcase in to do some studying, since he would be out of classes for a few days. The morning had gone by so fast while Bradford was studying. He jumped up and rushed to the kitchen to start cooking dinner for his new family he was so grateful to have, thanking God for his wonderful blessings he had given to him. It was time to go get Marcus from the bus stop. Bradford checked on Nikki before he left the house. She was sound asleep. He kissed her on the cheek, then pulled the blanket on her. He walked down the street going to the bus stop. Bradford had a big smile on his face, the joy that he had finally becoming a family man and studying to be a preacher man. Marcus got off the bus saying, "Daddy!" "Daddy!" Marcus liked saying that word because his biological dad died before Marcus was even born. Bradford picked him up and put him on his shoulders to walk home.

Marcus asked, "Where is mommy?" Bradford said, "She is home in bed sound asleep, she went to the dentist this morning and her medication makes her very sleepy. When we get home we will have to be quiet so that we won't wake her up. "Okay son?" Bradford explained. "Yes sir, daddy." Marcus said. When they went in the apartment, Nikki was sitting in the living room on the sofa, watching TV with her sleeping clothes on. Bradford and Marcus were really surprised to see her sitting there. Bradford asked, "Sweetheart, what are you doing up out of the bed?" Marcus ran over to give his mom a hug. Nikki explained. "Well honey, something was smelling so good in the kitchen, the aroma woke me up. What are you cooking that smells so good?" She asked. Bradford replied, "Dinner, Sweetheart." "I can't wait until it is done, because it smells so good," Nikki added. "I sure hope it tastes as good as it smells," Bradford replied.

Nikki and Marcus sat on the sofa and talked about what he had learned at school. Bradford went to the bathroom to wash his hands so he could go and finish dinner. Shortly after Bradford went into the kitchen, he asked Nikki and Marcus to go wash up because dinner was ready to be served, Marcus quickly jumped off the sofa and grabbed his Mommy's hands and helped her off the sofa. They went to the bathroom anxiously washing their hands, they were ready to dig into some good food that Bradford had prepared. Bradford had set up the plate settings on the card table they used as their dining room table. Everyone sat at the table, they all held hands as Bradford gave thanks to God for his wife, son, and the food that they were about to eat. Everyone enjoyed their dinner, Nikki raved to Bradford about how delicious the food was. Marcus said, "Daddy yum, yum this is good food." Bradford was very grateful to have Nikki and Marcus as his family, they would be the first family.

Everyone finished their dinner. Bradford told Nikki to go lay back down or to go sit back down on the sofa and watch TV. He told her that he and Marcus would put the leftovers up and clean the kitchen for her. Afterwards, I will help Marcus get his things together for school tomorrow, so sit back and relax and when we finish, Marcus will come and say good night. I will also read him a good night book and tuck him in for the night. Nikki sat back on the sofa and relaxed like her husband had suggested for her to do. While sitting there, she started thanking God for her preacher man that he had blessed her with. She was so grateful for the God-fearing, tall, dark, and handsome man with a briefcase she had prayed for so many years. She smiled to herself talking to God saying, "Lord, I was not praying for Bibles to be in the briefcase, when praying for the briefcase being a preacher's wife was nowhere in my mind at all." Nikki continued talking to God and smiling saying, "My plans was to be a doctor's wife, attorney's wife, or a CEOs wife, my prayers were answered, I just learned to be specific from here on out.

Nikki thought that one day she would be able to share her story and to teach that when you pray for something or for someone you have to be specific in what you are asking for. Nikki said, "Thank you God for my preacher man!" Bradford had a joyful time with Marcus, now it was time for bed. Bradford sent Marcus into the living room to give his Mommy a good night kiss. Nikki asked, "Did you have fun helping your Daddy clean the kitchen?" Marcus said, "Yes ma'am and Daddy got my clothes out for school tomorrow, helped me get my bath, helped me get dressed for bed and read some of my favorite good night books. Nikki gave him a big hug and kiss saying, "Sweet dreams, good night my son, Mommy loves you."

Bradford walked in the bedroom with Marcus and had him to get on his knees so he could teach him how to pray to God before he gets in bed. Marcus asked, "Daddy, why do I have to get on my knees?" "For two to pray to God, I am teaching you that we must thank God for being with us throughout the day and ask him to watch over us while we sleep, and to wake us up in the morning to start our day. We must thank God for everything in Jesus' name. Amen. This is why you are on your knees before bed Marcus." Bradford explained. Marcus got up and said, "I love you daddy. Good night!" Marcus jumped in the bed; Bradford pulled the blanket up and tucked Marcus in for the night. Bradford walked into the living room, feeling like he had never felt before, tired but grateful for his family.

Nikki looked up and saw Bradford coming in the room looking very tired. She said, "Honey, I am so sorry you have to be doing all of this because I am not able to do it right now. Nikki said, "Thank you my King, my dear husband, thank you so much." Bradford said, "No problem my Queen, my beautiful wife." They both laughed as she reached up for him to come join her on the sofa. The days passed and Nikki's mouth healed, the family was so happy everything was becoming normal for Bradford, Nikki, and Marcus, the first family.

TRICKS OF THE ENEMY

One thing that always happens whenever the devil sees that God's children has a happy home; he works to inject chaos to the marriage. Nikki had her work schedule changed, so she would be home with her family in the mornings and evenings. After a few weeks went by, she started to notice that she was not making the tips that she was used to making before she got married. She was no longer getting the evening dinner rush tips. Her new schedule started when the lunch rush was ending, and her shift was over just as the dinner rush started getting busy. One day she went home, and totaled up all her tips for the week, surprisingly, she did not even make $20 in tips. Nikki was so mad that she didn't have the money that she was used to making.

Nikki was stomping through the apartment when Bradford got home. He asked, "What's wrong sweetheart, did something happened at work?" Nikki went off and said as she was stomping through the apartment, "Yes, something happened at work." I used to make at least $300 Thursday through Sunday and I have worked for a week straight and I didn't even have $20, that's what's wrong!" Bradford stood there in awe, knowing that he had come home between classes to get some gas money from Nikki, to get back to his night classes. He thought to himself, *the way she is carrying on, I'm not asking her for anything.*

Bradford stood there listening to Nikki go on and on about not having any money in her pocket. She was not used to having empty apron pockets. Bradford looked at her and walked out the door to get some air. He went outside trying to keep his cool, thinking, *that woman just don't know who she's stomping at, she is in there acting just like a little brat.* Nikki is in the apartment thinking; *I did not get married to have no money, because I had money being a single mom.* Bradford being a man of God, prayed about what was happening between him and his new wife. He saw how Satan was going to try and make this money issue a big marital fight. Bradford continued praying, asking God for the right direction to handle what was going on in his marriage before he went back into the apartment. Nikki was very upset because she liked to spend money and now, she did not have any, and she blamed her new husband and that wasn't good. Bradford went back into the apartment and told Nikki to come and sit down. Nikki kindly did what Bradford suggested for her to do. He told her that he was going to the 66 books of the Bible to see what the word of God had to say to help this problem that they were having in their marriage. Nikki said, "Okay." Bradford went to the scriptures being directed by the Holy Spirit, Nikki sat and listened to what Bradford read to her. As he read, Nikki began to calm down and Bradford started to calm down too. Bible reading is one aspect of spiritual intimacy that can have an amazing impact on a couple's sense of togetherness. The scriptures Bradford had read truly helped the newlyweds.

The honey was back on the moon again. Nikki was so grateful that Marcus was at her sister's house on that day. After they settled down from honeymooning, they talked and realized that they needed a bigger place to live because it was time to put their apartment belongings under one roof; they needed somewhere they may be able to call home. Shortly after they started looking, God blessed them to find a house not far from the Bible College and Marcus's preschool. The house was a ranch-style home, it had three bedrooms, a bathroom, living room, kitchen, and a full basement with a big backyard for Marcus to play. They thanked God for blessing them with a house they could call home.

Bradford rounded up his preacher friends and Nikki rounded up her cousins so that moving into their home would be a smooth transition. The newlyweds were very thankful for the love and support they received from their family and friends. Nikki asked their support team to put everything from the two apartments in specific places, so once she started to decorate, everything would already be in place. Nikki let Bradford know that she was going to get some food to feed him and the workers. She gave him a kiss and headed to run some errands. Before she drove off, she went back inside the house to call Lois and asked her to bring Marcus home to their new house, also requesting Lois to help her serve the workers with food. Lois happily replied, "We will be there in about one hour." "Ok great, I should be back home with the food before then, stay safe sister, I'll see you in a little bit." Nikki said. She went to the store and bought everything she would need to feed her preacher man and their family and friends, that had showed up to help. Just as she was getting the food out of the bags, she heard her sister knocking on the door saying, "I'm coming in Nikki." "Come on in Lois, I'm in the kitchen." Nikki yelled. By that time, Marcus pulled away from his auntie and ran to where he heard his Mommy's voice. Marcus said, "Hi mommy!" Nikki bent down and gave her baby boy a big hug and kiss saying, "Welcome home Marcus, this is our new house, and you have a big backyard to play in!" Marcus was very excited to have a spacious home with a big backyard.

Lois asked her sister what she needed her to do. Nikki requested for her to organize the plates, plastics, napkins, and cups and place them at the end of the table, because the food would be set up buffet style. Lois said, "Wow sister, that's a great idea!" Nikki agreed, "Yes, less work for us." They both laughed. Nikki explained, "Once everything is set up for them to come and eat, I will give you a tour of the house." Marcus asked his Mommy if he could go outside and play in his new backyard. She told him that would be fine, and I will call you when I fix your plate. Lois finished her assignment and the two of them put the food on the table.

Lois decided to fill the cups with sweet tea so all they needed to do was get in line, fix their plates, pick up their drinks and find a place to sit. Bradford and the workers had a variety of tasks to complete to get the house fully set up. Once she found Bradford, she told him that lunch was ready. Bradford was very appreciative saying, "Sounds great sweetheart, I will go around and get everyone and meet you in the kitchen." Bradford went rounding up everyone, telling them that it was lunchtime. Bradford said, "My honey asked us to wash our hands and come to the kitchen and eat." They all agreed saying, "Okay, let's go and eat!" Once everyone was in the kitchen, Nikki asked, "Bradford could you please give thanks for the food?" Everyone bowed their heads as Bradford blessed the food, thanked God for their new home, their family and friends that were helping them, and the food that was prepared by his wife and sister-in-law in Jesus' name. They all said, "Amen." Nikki asked Bradford to start the buffet line at a particular spot for a steady flow. One of Bradford's preacher friends said, "Man your wife has our lunch laid out for us." Several of the workers were in total agreement as they happily filled their plates with good food for the soul. Nikki took pride in making sure that the workers felt appreciated for the time they took out of their day to help her, and Bradford make their house a home.

WELCOME TO PLEASURE PALACE

Bradford thanked God for his wife and hearing the workers complimenting her, it made him feel good knowing that she was his wife. They were impressed on how nice and organized she had their lunch set up. Once Nikki and Lois saw that the guys didn't need anything else, they took a tour of the house. The two of them walked downstairs to the basement. Nikki peeked out the window to check on Marcus playing in the backyard. He was having so much fun playing alone. Nikki told Lois that she was going to ask Bradford if she could invite their cousin down to stay with them and in return, he could do his handiwork on their basement. This way he would be able to start a new life in a new city. Lois said, "That sounds great Nikki. You are always thinking about helping others."

Nikki explained, "I think it would be good for him to have a new start, and once he's established, then he would be able to get his own place." Nikki mentioned to Lois that she knew a nice single woman that was around the same age as their cousin, and prayerfully if Bradford agreed for him to come, she would introduce them to each other. "Ok, Nikki, the matchmaker." Lois chuckled. "Okay Lois, let's look at other sections of the house because I'm getting excited about planning our cousin's future." Nikki expressed. The two of them went upstairs, walking from room to room while Nikki explained to her sister how she wanted each room to be decorated. Lois thought Nikki had great design ideas. After touring, they walked around to the backyard to get Marcus. Nikki said, "Come on son, it is time to go and eat."

Marcus was having so much fun, he did not want to come in. Nikki told him after you eat you may go back out to play. The three of them walked back in the house and went to the bathroom to wash their hands, on their way Nikki saw Bradford and his workers throwing their plates away. She asked, "Did you guys get everything that you needed?" Everyone told her that everything was delicious and thanked her for the lunch. Bradford said, "Sweetheart we thank you, but we got to get back to work before our food settles and if that happens, nobody will want to work, right guys," Bradford asked. They all agreed and said, "Yes, come on and let's get on it!" They finished up the house, it was set up just like Nikki had asked Bradford and the crew to put it together. All the furniture was placed where Nikki had asked. All she had to do now was go through the boxes and decorate their new home. Bradford, Nikki, and Lois walked their friends and family out to their cars and thanked them for all the work that they had done for them and said their goodbyes. Lois said, "Family, I'm going to go home and let the first family enjoy their new home." She told them goodbye and gave them a hug as they walked her to her car to leave.

Home sweet home! Bradford, Nikki, and Marcus, the first family was in their new home that God had blessed them with. Weeks had gone by, as they were settling in their new home, Nikki went to Bradford and suggested that they should start working on giving Marcus a sibling, a brother or sister, whichever God blesses them with. Bradford agreed saying, "Sounds good to me, come on and meet me in Pleasure Palace and we can get started, before Marcus gets home from school." Nikki laughed and said, "Bradford what a great idea, I am on my way." Bradford and Nikki really wanted to give Marcus a brother or sister, so they started honeymooning day and night.

Months and months went by, and nothing was happening, Nikki was not getting pregnant. Bradford and Nikki made doctor's appointments. Bradford's appointment was first, his test came back fine. Bradford was relieved that he was not shooting blanks as he rubbed his forehead while smiling inside. Now he was praying that the good news would be the same for his sweetheart. Nikki's appointment came, instead of the doctor saying everything was fine, he put Nikki on some vitamins and sent her home with a temperature chart. This chart was to keep up with her temperature every morning and when it hits the target temperature, that's the time Bradford and Nikki should come together in Pleasure Palace. One morning Nikki had gotten Marcus off to school, when she returned home, she heard Bradford taking a shower because he had early classes that morning.

Nikki remembered she had forgotten to check her temperature, so she rushed to the bedroom and sat down on her side of the bed; on the nightstand was her note pad and thermometer. She sat there for a minute to calm down because she was very anxious. She had rushed out that morning and had forgotten to do her morning routine by checking her temperature. Once she was calm, she put the thermometer in her mouth and waited for the beeping sound, once she heard the beeping, she pulled the thermometer out of her mouth and looked and checked the numbers. She jumped from the bed and ran to the bathroom door shouting out to Bradford, "It is time. It is time!" Bradford opened the bathroom door and asked, "It is time for what?" Nikki said to Bradford, "It is time for you Big Willie and the twins to meet me in the bedroom, where I will be holding my toes up in the air and my legs will spread wide open like a peace sign.

Bradford grabbed his towel and couldn't get out of the bathroom fast enough, almost slipping and sliding on the floor, saying, "We are on our way!" Bradford and Nikki laughed with joy. Later, Bradford went back to finish getting ready for class, leaving Nikki sound asleep in bed. Bradford looked at himself in the mirror thinking, *the vitamins that Nikki was taking was putting a whooping on him,* while patting himself, thanking God that it was a good whooping. Bradford was not complaining, smiling and appreciative of his blessings, he continued to get dressed, went to the bedroom and kissed Nikki on the forehead.

Bradford got in the car and before pulling off leaving for school, he had to pause a moment to give a Thanksgiving praise to God for all the blessing he was getting. Bradford wanted to let God know he was not ungrateful for the blessings. Every opportunity Bradford had; he was going to give God the praise. After the praise, he said, "Amen," and was on his way to class. Nikki got up from her nap and took a long, hot bath. While she was soaking, she was thanking God for all her blessings that he had given her. Nikki was so grateful to become a soldier in God's army. After she finished talking and praying to God, she got out of the bathtub, got dressed and was on her way to her part-time job. Nikki was loving her new name, Nikki Barlowe, she couldn't believe God had answered her prayers. The Barlowe family were doing well adjusting and becoming one in marriage. They were grateful for each other, Marcus, family and friends' support and their new home. The newlyweds continued to stay on the honeymoon because they never wanted the honey to fall off the moon.

One Saturday morning after having a big breakfast Nikki had prepared for the family, Marcus went to the backyard and played on his swing set that the neighbors next door had given him. The neighbors would watch Marcus from their patio playing by himself, so one day they knocked on their front door and introduced themselves as the neighbors next door. They told us that they would like to give our son the swing set that was in their backyard. They stated that their children were grown and gone and didn't seem like they would be getting any grandchildren soon, so they wanted to give the swing set to the little fellow that they watch playing by himself from their patio. They said, "Maybe have your friends come over, and you can lift the swing set from our yard to yours." Nikki and Bradford were overjoyed and thanked their neighbors for being very kind. They agreed that they would ask their friends to come and help move the swing set for Marcus.

REST IN HEAVENLY PEACE

Nikki quit her job and started college with Bradford. She was happy because the classes offered many benefits, and she was able to take classes that allowed her to meet other preacher's wives. She started out with the basic classes; her first semester's grades were very good. She was proud of herself, and her preacher man was proud of her too. During the second semester Nikki took mandatory classes, such as, the role of a preacher's wife, speech and speaking classes, couple's classes, and other classes to prepare the preacher's wives to get ready for the mission's field.

Brother and Sister Maine were great instructors, they had been on many missionary trips, saving souls for Christ. They had given Nikki and Bradford premarital counseling before they had gotten married at the Justice of the Peace. Nikki was happy for them, but she was still adjusting to being a preacher's wife and had no desire to go to the mission's field. Although it taught you what true selflessness looks like, the needs can be overwhelming and sobering. There was no running water, and you had to make your own soap to bathe. These experiences were very humbling, and a true testament of how good God had been to Bradford and Nikki.

The newlyweds had been enjoying and adjusting to life under one roof. Bradford was relaxing in the basement watching football and Nikki was cleaning up the kitchen. While wiping down the refrigerator, she noticed the calendar on the side of the refrigerator where she kept up with Marcus' school activities. She saw a date and went to her bedroom, sat down on the side of the bed, picked up her temperature note pad that had a calendar in the back, where she kept up with her monthly menstrual cycles. Nikki looked and said, "Oh my!" She asked herself, *how did I let this get passed me?* Nikki stood up and ran down the basement stairs, yelling, "Bradford, look!" "What am I looking at?" He asked. "This is my temperature calendar. The date I have marked for my cycle to start and what the date is today?" She asked. Bradford looked and said, "That was three days ago." Nikki explained, "No, it was three weeks ago, and I am never late for my cycles." Nikki was super excited, singing, "Bradford, we have a baby on the way!" Bradford responded, "Yes, we have a baby on the way!"

Bradford picked Nikki up saying, "We did it! We did it! We made a baby. Thank You Lord! Thank You Lord!" Bradford was very grateful and excited, he wanted to tell the world. Nikki said, "Let's tell Marcus after I go to the doctor to confirm, then we will tell our family and friends." Bradford agreed by saying, "Ok, sweetheart." Monday morning after Marcus had gone to school and Bradford had left for his morning classes, Nikki called her doctor to make an appointment to confirm her pregnancy. Nikki got off the phone with so much joy and excitement, thanking God for blessing her and Bradford to have a baby on the way, a sibling for Marcus. Nikki made the appointment around Bradford's lunchtime so that they could go together. Bradford picked her up at their home and they went to the appointment, both were smiling from ear-to-ear, thanking God silently in their minds saying to each other as they walked into the doctor's office, "We did it, we have a baby on the way!"

The couple had a wonderful doctor's appointment. A baby was truly on the way. Nikki and Bradford got a chance to hear a little something that the doctor said was the heartbeat. Two weeks after Nikki's first doctor's appointment she woke up out of her sleep around the crack of dawn in so much pain. Bradford heard her weeping and immediately asked her what was wrong. "We need to go to the hospital as soon as I can get dressed," Nikki said. Once they got Marcus up, they headed to the ER. Bradford pulled up to the door and ran inside asking for someone to come help his wife, because she was in a lot of pain. Help came and they pushed Nikki into one of the ER rooms and started to check her vitals, to determine the issue. Sadly, the pain that Nikki endured was because she was having a miscarriage. Bradford was standing in the waiting area where the nurse had taken them. He was pacing the floor with Marcus in his arms when he thought to himself, *I need to call family members and friends to ask if they would say a prayer for Nikki.* Just as he was finishing up calling everyone, the doctor came in and told Bradford what was happening to Nikki. Bradford asked, "Where's my wife? What is wrong with her?" The doctor replied, "Bradford, your wife is physically fine, but she miscarried the baby." He said, "Come and follow me and I will take you and your son to her room."

Once the doctor took them in to see Nikki, Marcus ran and hopped in bed with his mommy. Marcus asked, "Mommy, Mommy, what's wrong?" As the tears rolled from her eyes, she told Marcus that his little brother Darren had went back to baby heaven with God. The doctor told the family, "On behalf of the doctors and hospital staff, we are truly sorry for your loss." Bradford thanked the doctor for taking good care of his wife. He walked him to the door asking in a quiet voice if his wife was going to be ok. The doctor replied, "Yes, she is going to be just find." Bradford went and stood beside the bed and leaned over and kissed Nikki on the forehead. "Honey, I am so sorry I miscarried the baby, our "Love Child" we worked so hard to conceive." Nikki said.

Bradford told her that he was so grateful to God that she was alright. Marcus had fallen asleep at the foot of his mommy's bed. Bradford said. "Wake up son, time to go home and get ready for school. We will come back after you get out of school, so you can spend more time with your mommy." Marcus said, "Yes sir." He gave his mommy a hug and a kiss. Bradford gave her a kiss and said, "Sweetheart, I will be back after I get Marcus off to school." Bradford and Nikki were truly learning what the judge had them to state in their vows, "In sickness and in health," and they had not been married very long. Nikki stayed in the hospital for three days, while she was there, she did a lot of talking to God; that is when she wasn't being cared for by the nurses and doctors.

The day that Nikki came home, Lois and Jason got together with their family and friends, they went over to visit with Bradford and Nikki, to give the Barlowe family some love, laughter, and good food. Jason and Lois were good at bringing joy into their family and friends' lives. They pulled up in front of the house and saw all the cars, and family and friends standing in the yard with smiles, balloons, food, and drinks. Bradford had no idea about the surprise welcome home from the hospital party, for Nikki and the family. Everyone knew how much they wanted to give Marcus a sibling. Family and friends stood hand and hand on each side of the sidewalk as The Barlowe family walked through to the front door. Once Bradford let Nikki and Marcus in the house, she turned around and said, "Everyone come on in so we can eat and have a wonderful and glorious time! Let's give Jason and Lois a big hand clap for putting this fun time together for me and my family."

     They had so much fun laughing, eating, talking, and playing cards. The party was over and now it was time to move forward, without Nikki having the baby in her arms. For better or worst Bradford and Nikki now have experienced the death of their love child. They knew that God wanted little Darren back with him in baby Heaven, that's what gave them comfort knowing that one day, God would bless The Barlowe family with more siblings for Marcus.

THE WEDDING CEREMONY

Bradford and his family started attending a church in town. He wanted to be more involved in the church services. The college church already had their people in specific positions and Bradford had started to become tired of just sitting in the congregation, keeping the pews warm. The church in town offered Bradford $400.00 a month for support and Bradford would also be able to preach once a month and teach Bible study on Wednesday's. Everything started to run smoothly for Bradford and his family. Everyone was doing well in church, college and Marcus continued to do well in school.

Nikki had some afternoon time after finishing her classes that semester, so she decided to get a part-time job to have some extra money. The extra money would help her along with what she had been saving from her college benefits. The extra money would also help them start planning the wedding ceremony that Bradford said they would have at the church. Nikki had always joked with her cousin Jason about getting married at this beautiful church that they walked passed almost every day. Nikki's first check, she went shopping for a wedding dress. After shopping around, she finally found the perfect dress that she was able to put on layaway.

Nikki was so excited about her beautiful wedding dress. She smiled all the way down the mall's hallway. Just as she was getting ready to exit the mall, she saw a jewelry store with signs advertising, "Sale, Sale, and Sale!" Nikki loved to see that word, because she was looking for a gold watch for her preacher man. Nikki browsed around the store for this gold and diamond watch. The regular price was $400.00 but the sale price was 75% off. Nikki had hit the jackpot! She hurried to get the salesperson to ask about layaway options. The salesman said it was offered so she put the watch on layaway for Bradford a graduation gift. As Nikki walked to the car, she thanked God for the favor she had just been granted, the good deals on the dress and watch.

It was getting close to the big day. Invitations had been sent out and everything was set. Nikki and Bradford were excited because graduation and their wedding ceremony was on the same day. They knew it was going to be an extremely busy day but with their family and friends' support, they would cherish every moment. Nikki's favorite saying, "It will be a wonderful, glorious and joyful day!" Family members came from all over to attend the graduation and wedding ceremony. Only a handful showed up for Bradford's graduation. He was a little disappointed, but he didn't have time to stay upset, because he and Nikki had to rush back home and start getting things together for their wedding ceremony. Everything went just as planned, like clockwork, very smooth. It was a beautiful, sunny day in July. The church sanctuary was lit with gorgeous heart-shaped candelabras, one large, one medium-sized and two small ones on each side, adorned with royal blue, gold and white flowers placed in the pulpit.

Nikki's wedding gown was white lace, sheer long sleeves, V-neck sheer with crystals and sequins. The shape of the wedding gown was like Cinderella in fairy tales. The bride complimented her gown with a white, oval laced veil, sequins, and crystals that beautified the top of her head. The white laced train was extended with sequins and crystals. Nikki's hair was pulled back into a beautiful bridal bun. Her medium-sized bridal bouquet featured a beautiful array of fresh white roses with a hint of blue delphinium flowers, accented with gold-glazed leaves and streamers. The ushers placed a white runner down the aisle for the beautiful bride to grace her guests.

Bradford looked very handsome in his white tuxedo with a white tailcoat and a royal blue and gold boutonniere. The wedding cake was 7 tiers with stairs on each side leading to 2 tiers, the colors were accented with white and royal blue roses and gold leaves. Seven bridesmaids wore beautiful, floor length royal blue satin dresses, escorted by seven groomsmen in their black tuxedo, accented with a royal blue and gold boutonniere. The flower girls looked like little princesses wearing their pearl-colored lace Cinderella style dresses. Last but not least, Marcus adored the crowd looking handsome in his white tuxedo with an elongated white tailcoat, and royal blue and gold boutonniere identical to his Daddy Bradford.

The ceremony was breathtaking! After Nikki and Bradford shared their wedding nuptials, prayer, and blessings, as it was time for Bradford to kiss his bride, the preacher had to clear his throat for Bradford and Nikki to stop kissing. This brought joy and laughter to their guests and wedding party. As the wedding ceremony came to an end, the wedding party departed the sanctuary and went across the street to take pictures in front of the beautiful over-sized water fountain. Bradford and Nikki were happy and very thankful that family and friends attended their ceremony and showered them with money and gifts. Marcus, looking so handsome in his tuxedo, was happy because he received gifts that day. Bradford was truly happy to be able to share his special day with his best friend that had come to be best man. The year prior, Bradford was asked to be his best man in his wedding. Everyone went home happy, and their stomach filled with wonderful delicacies after the reception.

Sunday morning came and it was time for church. Bradford and Nikki really liked going to their new church. Nikki loved seeing her preacher man preaching on his assigned Sundays. She also loved watching Bradford teach Wednesday night Bible Study. Everything was going well, even the preacher and the brothers of the church were encouraging Bradford on how well he was doing and blessing the congregation. Bradford was thankful for the opportunity. After church, Bradford and his family headed to Bradford's favorite seafood restaurant. They loved to order the seafood platter filled with shrimp, fish, crab cakes, crabs, fried oysters, and clams served with their favorite two sides, a baked potato with butter and sour cream, and a tossed salad. They always enjoyed family dinners together. Bradford wanted to take his love for the ministry to another level. He started looking for a church home to be the Lead Pastor. He started sending out resumes to churches that were looking for a preacher. Nikki was very excited about Bradford venturing out to be a full-time minister. She knew that whenever Bradford got the opportunity to lead a church, they would be well taken care of. Nikki had witnessed this all her life growing up as a child.

It was wonderful that they could go to the new church and get support until Bradford heard from the resumes he had sent out. That week Nikki and Marcus went to the mall to get Bradford's graduation gift that was long overdue to be out. It was a nice gesture that the jewelry store did for Nikki to extend her layaway time. Once they arrived at the jewelry store, Nikki asked the salesperson if they could gift wrap the watch. Nikki and Marcus were very happy that they would be able to bless Bradford with a beautiful gold and diamond watch for all his hard work.

CHURCH FOLKS

It was Sunday morning, time to get ready for church. This was the Sunday that Bradford was scheduled to preach. It made Bradford feel good that morning because a lot of his family were still in town, and they were at church to hear him preach. Bradford got up to preach and looked out into the congregation and saw all the out-of-town family and friends. He was very thankful they had come to hear him preach. Seeing them there took all the disappointments he had for them not attending his graduation. As Bradford was preaching, Nikki listened and admired her preacher man. She thought he was very handsome in his three-piece suit and tie, golden cuff links, and hair groomed to perfection, standing in the pulpit blessing the congregation with a mighty word from God. Nikki couldn't wait to give Bradford his graduation gift, she knew that would be the icing on the cake.

Nikki snapped back quickly into the word, asking God to forgive her from daydreaming during the church service. After church Bradford and his family, and his extended family went out to dinner. Since Bradford had graduated, he started sending resumes to different churches for a full-time preaching position. Nikki decided to ask for more hours at her part-time job, so she could help the family, but she was sure hoping that a church would call him very soon. She wanted to live the life she had fantasized about. Nikki learned that it is not always her timing, but God's perfect timing. Being a Christian, she knew that things wouldn't always be in her favor, but she must continue to serve and obey God.

Nikki's new work schedule worked out well for her and her family. The next Saturday, Nikki was off work, she and Marcus were excited to give Bradford his graduation gift. She wanted to give it to him in time to wear the next Sunday, which happened to be the Sunday for him to preach again.

That Sunday morning after breakfast, the family was ready to head out for church and Nikki told Marcus to go to his room and get the gift for his Daddy. Bradford was sitting on the bed, his eyes opened wide as Marcus was coming down the hallway. He asked, "Son, what is it?" Nikki was so excited she captured the Kodak moment with her camera. Marcus said, "Daddy, it is your graduation gift from me and Mommy. You got to open it, Daddy." Bradford got up and sat down on the sofa to open the gift. Nikki asked Marcus to go stand by his Daddy so she could take a picture of him giving his Daddy the graduation gift.

Bradford opened the gift and saw a stylish gold and diamond watch. He was overjoyed to see what his wife and son had gotten him for graduation. "Thank you very much! I love it!" Bradford said, while putting it on. Nikki was happy that it fit perfectly. Bradford gave Nikki and Marcus a big hug and kiss and thanked them again. It was time to get ready for church, Bradford wore his new watch to enhance his dress attire. Sunday school was wonderful, and the church service was on fire with the spirit. The praise and worship, prayer warriors, preaching of the Word, and the entire church service was spirit filled.

Nikki was sitting watching her preacher man preaching a very powerful sermon, it was a lot of hand clapping and hollering, "Amen." Nikki admired how Bradford's watch accented his suit, smiling and thanking God she was able to do that for her preacher man. After church, everyone was refreshed ready to take on the week ahead, applying the sermon lessons that they had gotten from the preacher man, Bradford. Things were just going too good for Satan, he had to find a weak link to use and that is exactly what he did. It was time for Wednesday Night Bible Study, time for Bradford to teach and he was so ready, because he was still on a spiritual high from his sermon on Sunday. When they pulled into the church parking lot one of the brothers was standing there. Nikki said to Bradford, "I wonder why he is standing there, looks like he is waiting for someone," not knowing it was them he was waiting to speak with.

Bradford and his family got out of the car and walked across the church parking lot. As they were getting ready to walk through the door the brother told Bradford that he needed to speak with him. He said, "Okay." Bradford told Nikki to go on in the church building and he would be in after he finished talking with the brother. Nikki's brain was always thinking, wondering as she and Marcus went to the pew what that brother wanted to talk with Bradford about. She had a feeling that it was not good news whatever it was, because that brother always seemed to be very friendly, but today it looked like something was wrong. Satan had found his weak link to crush Bradford's spirit. Bradford and the brother was still standing outside, when Bradford proceeds to ask what was going on that we must be outside to talk. The brother told Bradford that he would not be teaching Bible Study tonight and that all the brothers wanted to meet with him after class, and any questions can be asked then. "Okay," Bradford said. Bradford went inside to join his family wondering what was really going on because he hadn't ever seen this brother act that way.

Bradford sat down beside Nikki and Marcus and whispered in her ear that he would not be teaching Bible Study tonight; "The brothers want to have a meeting with me after Bible Study is over." She said, "Really, I wonder what that's all about," with a worried look on her face. Bradford said, "I don't know but only time will tell Sweetheart," taking her by the hand saying, "We have God on our side, whatever it may be he will work it out. Nikki responded, "Yes, I agree, he will!" After Bible study was over, Bradford went back where the brothers were and he asked the question again, "What is this meeting all about?" The same brother that was waiting on Bradford in the parking lot was the one that answered saying, "The church will be cutting off support for you starting tonight." Bradford stated, "It was in my agreement that I would teach and preach for this congregation until I relocate where the Lord wants to plant me, and now you are saying that I will not be receiving any more support. "Is it something I said or did?"

The brother responded, "We decided if you can go out and purchase a $400.00 gold and diamond watch, you do not need any support from us. All the brothers saw the watch." Bradford was livid inside but kept his composure. He explained to the brothers that his wife purchased the watch as a graduation gift for him. Bradford stayed positive and addressed the preacher and the brothers of how much joy he had working with them. Bradford was upset, but he knew where his help comes from, not man, but God. Sadly, this is how Satan uses the weak link to have everybody doing just what he or she wants. Many of the brothers had no idea what had happened to Bradford. On their way home, Nikki asked, "Bradford, what was the meeting about?" He said, "I will tell you once we put Marcus in bed." Bradford didn't talk church business around Marcus.

Nikki could tell by Bradford's facial expression that it was not a good meeting. Once Nikki tucked Marcus in for the night, she walked into the living room where Bradford was sitting on the sofa. She sat down beside him and held his hands, and he told her that Satan had started to attack their ministry. She asked, "What do you mean?" He told her that the preacher and brothers had decided to stop their monthly support. They had noticed the watch that you and Marcus had given me for my graduation gift. They wondered, if I could go out and buy a $400.00 watch, then they did not need to continue supporting us.

Nikki told Bradford I did not pay that much for your watch but if I did, it's nothing wrong with getting the best for the one you love. She asked, "What kind of people come up with their own conclusions and not know the facts of how and why you were wearing a $400.00 watch, and then break an agreement?" Bradford said, "I guess those are the people that attend church, doing what pleases them and not belonging to Christ, doing his will." Nikki was so upset asking, "What are we supposed to do?" "God will take care of us, just like he always has done," expressed Bradford. Nikki pulled her hand from Bradford and went outside to the patio because she needed to get some air. He said, "I will come with you." "No, please Bradford, I need to be by myself right now." Nikki storms out to the patio and sat down saying to herself, *what have I gotten myself into marrying this preacher.*

As soon as that statement came to her thoughts there was Satan, getting ready to use what Nikki had just thought making her a weak link. Nikki leaned her head back and looked at the stars and moon shining so brightly. Instead of her thanking God for the beautiful night, Satan took her somewhere else, captured her thoughts, taking her back to reminiscing about her past. Once Satan does that, he will have you saying, "Woulda, Coulda, Shoulda!" Satan wants to keep you from identifying with your current life, serving God.

Nikki thoughts went back to a past love named, Jefferson. They had a special relationship, their hands fit together just like a hand and glove, perfect. Thinking back, she remembered how she and Jefferson would lie on the hood of his car at night and look at the moon and stars until daybreak. They had so much in common, Satan continued to fuel the fire, and Nikki's thoughts were, *if only our relationship had lasted.* She was thinking that it was love and not lust between them. She believed that he broke off the relationship from the influence that was coming from others and not following his heart that he truly loved her. Satan was getting ready to continue to keep her thoughts going, when suddenly Bradford came out on the patio and said, "Sweetheart, I'm just coming out to check on you." Nikki felt guilty about what she had been thinking, so she asked God to forgive her for the thoughts she had about another man, while being married to Bradford.

GOD'S PERFECT TIMING

Nikki told Bradford, that she had calmed down and she agreed with him, that God will take care of them, just like he had always done. Nikki thought about what the Bible says in [Matthew 6:26]. Afterwards, she thought about what she had learned from that chapter and verse. Her mind was at ease to not worry about what was going to happen to them, since the church attenders had taken their support away. Satan does not want Nikki to take her thoughts back to God, he will just wait until she becomes the weak link again. Bradford sat down beside Nikki and told her he would be calling his friend, Brother Goodyear in the morning to tell him what had happened. This would be the test of faith for Bradford and Nikki. The next morning Nikki started breakfast, while she was preparing the meal, she thanked God for waking her and her family up to start another beautiful day. She asked again for forgiveness for what she had been thinking about last night. Nikki called the loves of her life in for breakfast. The family ate and Marcus headed off to school.

Just as Bradford was going to the phone it rang and it was for Nikki. It was the doctor's office calling to tell her that her annual test results came back just fine, but they had some good news from her blood work. Nikki asked, "What is the good news?" The nurse said, "You are going to have a baby!" Nikki was so excited to hear that. She got off the phone and ran to tell Bradford the good news. She told him, "We are going to have a brother or sister for Marcus!" Bradford said, "What did you say?" Nikki repeated herself, "We are going to have a baby!" Bradford was very excited, then he thought about their support that had been taken away. He did not let Nikki see the worry in him. He said, "Sweetheart, I need to go and make that phone call to Brother Goodyear, to let him know what has happened and maybe he can give me some direction on what I need to do." Nikki said, "Okay, and when you get off the phone, let me know so I can call Mother and Lois." "Okay." Bradford replied.

Nikki went to start getting ready for work. Before Bradford picked the phone up to call Brother Goodyear, Satan captured his thoughts. Bradford started wondering, *why did I leave my hometown and come to this place to get a degree in the ministry. I should have chosen another career.* He thought very quickly how giving his life to God, saved his life from a world of sinful doings. Satan didn't like Bradford telling him to get behind him, because he was going to serve God. Satan could not make Bradford a weak link, he also thought of the scripture [Matthew 6:26]. Bradford called Brother Goodyear and told him what had happened. How will Brother Goodyear help Bradford and his growing family? Find out in Volume 2 of Love or Lust! To be continued.

Q-DAB'S HELPFUL DATING HINTS

1. Share your faith and conviction to God
2. Communicate expectations
3. Consider each other's interest and hobbies
4. Always be honest

Q-DAB'S HELPFUL HINTS FOR NEWLYWEDS AND MARRIED COUPLES

4-K Formula

1. Keep God in front
2. Keep people out of your business
3. Keep the communication open
4. Keep the honey on the moon

This will promote togetherness and keep a smile on your face.

BIBLICAL REFERENCES

Being a single Mom was never the plan for many of us, however, God has a plan for your life no matter your circumstances. Sometimes you may feel inadequate or unequipped to have a relationship with God because of the mistakes you've made. In the Bible, you will see where Jesus hung with people that others may have thought wasn't deserving of his presence. It doesn't matter what you are going through, God wants you to trust him with your children, marriage, health, relationships, finances, goals, and aspirations, and especially your heart. **"And this same God who takes care of me will supply all your needs from his glorious riches, which have been given to us in Christ Jesus." [Philippians 4:19]**

Life is so full of surprises. We never know what blessings may be in store for us. Always have faith and trust in God. It is wonderful when you follow God's word which will lead you to your heart's desires. **"In all thy ways acknowledge him, and he shall direct thy paths." [Proverbs 3:6]**

No matter how hard it hurts, telling the truth is better than telling a lie. **"Now the Lord is the Spirit, and where the Spirit of the Lord is, there is freedom. And you will know the truth, and the truth will set you free" [John 8:32]**

Whatever trials and tribulations you may face in life always know that God is bigger than any problem. **"The Lord is on my side; I will not fear: what can man do unto me?" [Psalm 118:6]**

The only way we can truly have a pure heart is to give our lives to Christ and ask him to cleanse us from sin. **"Blessed are the pure in heart, for they shall see God" [Matthew 5:8]**

IN MEMORY

of

Family and Friends that cheered me on to finish my book

Mother
Mattie E. Clemons

Dad
Charley L. Clemons

Sister
Mattie L. Clemons Vaughn

Cousin/Brother
George L. Rowell

Mother in the Gospel
Sister LaVoyne Shields Worthey

Friend/Sister in Christ
Beatrice Morris

ACKNOWLEDGEMENTS

I would like to thank my husband and our children for being there supporting me every step of the way. I love you all very much.

Thank you to my biggest supporter, my cheerleader, my dear sister-in-law Alline (Bay) Bush. Thanks so much Sis.

Thank you to all my family and friends who have supported me throughout the years in writing my book. Your love and support are greatly appreciated.

Thank you to my readers and followers for your support. Have a wonderful, glorious, and joyful day!

ABOUT THE AUTHOR

Q-DAB is a wife, mother of three and grandmother of ten sweet and loving grandchildren, five princes and five princesses. She works along beside her husband ministering in the Church of Christ and serving in the community for over 38 years. She loves working with her church family and being a wonderful support for her Minister.

Q-DAB enjoys sharing ideas and executing assignments to uplift the name of Jesus with help from her sisters in Christ. During her leisure time, she loves golfing, fishing, gardening, indoor skydiving and being a fashion coordinator for herself, family, and friends.

LET'S CONNECT

Email: **Qdab.theauthor@yahoo.com**

Facebook: facebook.com/TheAuthorQ-DAB

BOOK SUMMARY

Nikki's infatuation with her secret crush took her down a journey filled with lust, secrets, lies, and an unexpected blessing that led her to relocate closer to her family. She was a waitress at the local diner and often prayed that God would send her a God-fearing, tall, dark, and handsome companion wearing a suit and carrying a briefcase.

As Nikki walked to her section to greet her customers, there sat the spitting image of the man of her dreams. The two made an undeniable connection which took their courtship full speed ahead, but there was still a mystery about her prince charming that made her realize to always be specific in your prayers, because you might just get what you ask for.

Made in the USA
Columbia, SC
01 September 2023